W

THE TOFF GOES TO MARKET

THE TOFF GOES TO MARKET

John Creasey

Chivers Press
Bath, England • G.K. Hall & Co.
Thorndike, Maine USA

This Large Print edition is published by Chivers Press, England, and by G.K. Hall & Co., USA.

Published in 1989 in the U.K. by arrangement with the author's estate.

Published in 1997 in the U.S. by arrangement with Harold Ober Associates Incorporated.

U.K. Hardcover ISBN 0–7451–8951–2 (Chivers Large Print)
U.S. Softcover   ISBN 0–7838–1991–9 (Nightingale Collection Edition)

The text of this Large Print edition is unabridged.
Other aspects of the book may vary from the original edition.

Set in 16 pt. New Times Roman.

Printed in Great Britain on acid-free paper.

British Library Cataloguing in Publication Data available

Library of Congress Cataloging-in-Publication Data

Creasey, John.
  The Toff goes to market / John Creasey.
    p. cm.
  ISBN 0–7838–1991–9 (lg. print : sc)
  1. Large type books.   I. Title.
[PR6005.R517T64   1997]
823′.912—dc20
                                          96–43100

CHAPTER ONE

THE TOFF DOES HIS DUTY

What would have happened had Lady Matilda Wirrington not been seized with violent cramps in the stomach, so severe and alarming that within twenty-four hours telegrams and telephone calls were being made to her many relatives, no one can predict with certainty. Certainly no one would have prophesied the erratic course of events in the next few days.

Had Lady Matilda died, the Toff probably would have returned to his unit immediately after the funeral; but she lived, talked, and thus lit the match which started the fire which developed from the little blaze of ptomaine poisoning *plus* into the conflagration of black market *minus*. The difference between *plus* and *minus* can be small but never insignificant.

At the time the Toff was stationed in Surrey. When he received the telegram he frowned and was hesitant, for he had no great regard for his aunt. Moreover, he knew that if there were a serious prospect that she would die a swarm of relatives would buzz about her sick-bed, most of them failing to conceal the hope that before she died she would indicate their share, if any, of her considerable fortune.

Most of his relatives nauseated the Toff.

1

It happened that he was Aunt Matilda's nearest blood-relative on the male side, and duty dictated an obvious course, but when he approached Colonel Travers he had more than a sneaking hope that he could not be spared.

Travers, a burnished whippet, killed this hope promptly.

'Yes, Rollison, of course. Can manage without you for a few days. Just had word we're staying here for at least another month.' Travers, who was never expansive but often informative, made a gurgling noise in his throat indicating that he was annoyed that the unit was to remain in England, and added: 'Where will you be staying?'

'My flat will find me,' said Rollison sadly.

'Tell you what,' said Travers. 'Littleton is going to take some papers to Whitehall for me.' He just contrived not to make 'Whitehall' a sneer. 'Go up with him. Save petrol, and save your time.'

Consequently, two hours after he had received the telegram but eight hours after it had been sent, Rollison presented himself at the front door of 7 Braddon Place, W.1. He was received by a white-haired servant who bowed frigidly.

'Hallo, Patton,' said Rollison. 'How is she?'

'Neither better, sir, nor worse.'

'So we have to be thankful.'

Rollison was led to the door of a large drawing-room which he knew well. He

2

imagined the room would be crowded, for a drone of conversation, which could not have been caused by a mere half-dozen, filtered through the closed door.

'Oh, Patton, telephone Jolly for me, will you,' asked Rollison, 'and tell him I'll be at the flat some time tonight?'

'Very good, sir.' Patton flung open the drawing-room door, and almost shouted in order to be heard above the cackle which confirmed Rollison's worst fears:

'Major the Hon. Richard Rollison!'

Perhaps four people, all near the door, looked up, and for an appreciable time the conversation continued unabated. Then a little woman with a shrill voice advanced with hand outstretched, and her voice pierced more ears than Patton's.

'Oh, Rolly, *darling*! So glad you have managed to get away!'

'Yes. Nice to see you,' murmured Rollison. Had he been in a better mood he would have been amused, for the conversation died away and most eyes turned towards him; he estimated fifteen pairs, seventy-five per cent of them feminine.

The only men were old, or youths not yet old enough for the Forces. There were a few youngish women in uniform, and by the fireplace—which was empty, for it was a hot August—sat a woman with a hardy face, luxuriant grey hair, and big and unblinking

3

grey eyes not unlike Rollison's.

Most of the fifteen or sixteen present greeted him; some heartily, some disapprovingly, some distantly. The little woman with the shrill voice, a cousin many times removed, clung to his arm; he knew that her tongue was often vitriolic when discussing him. In his family he was either the black sheep or the celebrity.

He disposed of his distant cousin with a murmured apology, passed between two men on the near side of the fireplace and reached the hardy-faced woman, who looked up at him without a smile. Unlike most of the other elderly females there, she was dressed in a gown of maroon-coloured satin; generally the colours were black or grey or navy blue, anticipatory of mourning.

'So you've come, have you?' Her voice was just a little too feminine to be mistaken for a man's. 'I wonder you took the trouble.'

'Oh, no trouble. Just a sense of duty.' He proffered cigarettes, and when she hesitated went on: 'Aunt Glory, if you're letting yourself be overwhelmed by this galaxy of heirs appalling, I'm finished with you. Smoke and be damned to them.'

Lady Gloria Hurst took a cigarette; her fingers were long, strong, and browned, like Rollison's.

'How's Aunt Matilda?' asked Rollison.

'Don't tell me you care,' said Aunt Glory tartly. 'If there's anything to be said in your

4

favour, Richard, it is that you're not a hypocrite. Not one of these'—she paused, and then enunciated clearly—'*scavengers* is interested in Matilda or anything but their share of her fortune. I think sometimes that the blood is so thin none of them will live to see the year out.'

'Too much inbreeding,' said Rollison judicially.

'Because your father married an actress do you think that made you a perfect specimen?' demanded Glory acidly.

'It just thickened my blood. If we go on like this much longer I shall think *you* haven't inquired how Matilda is.'

The grey eyes twinkled for the first time.

'That tongue of yours will get you into trouble one day. I think she's rather better. In fact,' added Lady Gloria, lowering her voice and pulling him a little nearer, 'I'm just holding my breath until Carruthers gives his final verdict. I think he'll say she's out of danger, and I'm longing to see their faces. All they'll have got out of it is a free tea; I'm damned if I'll find them a dinner. Let them use up their own rations.' She puffed vigorously at the cigarette. 'What's the Army like now, Richard?'

'Much as it always was, I imagine,' said Rollison.

Before he could go on the door opened again and Patton announced Dr Carruthers.

A gruff man, Carruthers, nearly seventy but

5

upright as any poker, bony-chinned, and with eyes of china blue. Rollison thought it one of the anomalies of life that Carruthers, whose diagnoses were always distressingly blunt, particularly when he suspected malingering, should become a successful Mayfair doctor.

Carruthers bored his way through the throng and a dozen anxious comments to reach Lady Gloria, Matilda's sister.

'She'll pull through,' Carruthers said, audibly enough for the whole room to hear. 'She'd like to see you, Richard, and you, Lady Gloria.' He turned aside to answer a question hurled at him in a shrill voice.

Rollison watched the faces of the relatives. Most were mask-like; here and there were examples of positive regret, and two people looked genuinely relieved.

Lady Gloria stood up; she was of a height with Rollison, who topped six feet, but that was partly due to her piled grey hair. She told the shrill voice and many others that she was sure they understood that it would be impossible to prepare a dinner for them all. Then she put an arm in Rollison's and commanded him to take her upstairs. In her other hand she carried an ebony walking-stick, for at sixty-nine she was recovering from a broken leg incurred while riding to hounds.

The door closed behind them.

'I'd like to know what they're saying and thinking,' said Lady Gloria. 'Rolly, what *is* the explanation of so many of the family being like that?'

'I've told you,' said Rollison. 'And, now we're alone, what was the matter with you? You haven't called me Richard since I was knee high.'

'I thought you weren't coming.'

'And you thought I ought?'

'Of course I did.' They went slowly up the stairs, and she did not speak again until they had reached the landing. Then she stood and faced Rollison. 'Rolly, don't be hard on Matilda. There was always more in her than she allowed you and the world to see. She's been very near Kingdom Come, or thinks she has. That's had a salutary effect.'

Rollison frowned. 'Just what are you driving at?'

'You'll see,' said Glory, and vouchsafed nothing more until they were in the enormous bedroom where Aunt Matilda was lying forlorn in a four-poster bed. By the window was a nurse, by the bed a maid.

Lady Matilda Wirrington had been a great beauty in her youth, and was one of the few whom age had not made less remarkable. Although the sudden illness had ravaged her complexion so that now it was pasty and blotchy, it was impossible not to realize that she was a handsome creature. She had silver-white hair, which Rollison knew was bleached, and fine blue eyes. They were narrowed, and

7

Rollison suspected that she had been through considerable pain.

She patted the side of her bed gently; her hand was thin and veiny.

'Hallo, Richard, it's nice of you to come.' Rollison smiled, bent down, and kissed her forehead. 'What has Glory been telling you?'

'Nothing; she's just been mysterious. But, Aunt, ought you to worry yourself now?'

'Whether I worry myself now or later it won't make any difference,' declared Matilda. 'Richard—*are* you a detective?'

The question so startled Rollison that he nearly gaped. Lady Gloria poked him in the ribs. He sat on the side of the bed, alert for the first time and also wary.

'I don't know whether "detective" is the word,' he said, 'but I have been able to help the police occasionally.' He was prepared to be told that Matilda thought she had been deliberately poisoned, and was already grappling with the possible suspects among the motley downstairs, when she gripped his hand with surprising strength and said in a low-pitched voice:

'It was my own fault, Richard. I knew I shouldn't have bought it.'

'Oh,' said Rollison blankly.

'He isn't often as dull as this, Matilda,' said Lady Gloria.

'Will you be quiet?' demanded her sister. 'Don't keep prodding him in the back, either.

Richard, I bought a case of tinned salmon two weeks ago, and opened the first tin yesterday for lunch. *That's* what caused it. Dr Carruthers knows it was the salmon, but he doesn't know it was out of a case.' She paused, and her narrowed eyes searched Rollison's face. 'Perhaps you don't realize, as you're in the Army—'

'I know that buying a case of tinned salmon is enough to have you fined a thousand pounds, and possibly earn you a prison sentence,' Rollison said.

'If you say "Whatsoever a man soweth that shall he also reap" I shall scream at you,' declared Matilda, obviously very much better in health yet sick with remorse born out of the fear of death. He recalled what Glory had said on the landing and knew now at what she had been driving. Yet he smiled reassuringly.

'I won't,' he promised. 'You seem to know it.'

'I always knew Glory was right about you,' said Matilda, 'but you are an annoying beast at times; you've often shoo'd me out of the flat to see one of those funny little friends of yours from the East End. If you prefer men like that to people of your own kind, that's not on *my* conscience. Richard, I wanted to talk to you, *quickly*, because if you are a detective you might be able to stop any more of that salmon being sold. If it nearly killed me—and I'm as strong as Glory—what will it do to other

9

people who buy cases?'

'You have a point,' admitted Rollison.

'Can you *do* anything?' demanded Matilda. Her face was a little flushed, her eyes were wider open and intensely blue as she clutched at Rollison's hand. 'Can you, Richard? I *can't* tell the police. Or—or I don't want to have to. I know I might be sent to prison and I couldn't bear it. I just couldn't bear it!'

The nurse approached firmly.

'I don't think you should talk any more, m'lady.'

'You mind your own business!' snapped Matilda. 'I asked the doctor if it was all right. Go away. Richard can you?'

'I might be able to help,' admitted Rollison, and slid a hand to his pocket. 'Supposing I can't, Aunt Mattie; what are you going to do?'

Glory prodded him in the ribs again.

'What can I do?' demanded Matilda slowly. 'I've been counting on you, Richard. I have really been *depending* on you. I don't think I could face prison, I'd rather die. But they *mustn't* sell any more of that salmon; I'm sure it will kill a lot of people. If you can't help me I'll have to tell the police.' She paused again, and the nurse stared vindictively at Rollison's profile, determinedly unimpressed by his good looks. 'Will you *try*, Richard? I can give you the address of the man I bought it from.'

'I'll try—I really will,' Rollison promised her. 'Don't get too worked up though; it might

10

have been one bad tin out of the gross, or however many were in the case. I've a lot of queer and unsocial habits,' he continued with a teasing smile, 'but I'll do my level best to keep the family escutcheon clean.'

He stood up, and Matilda said thinly:

'Glory knows where the rest of the tins are. Thank you, Richard; I *felt* that you wouldn't disappoint me.' She turned to the nurse and her smile was positively angelic. 'Give me my bag, nurse dear, will you please, and then I'll rest.'

The nurse brought her bag. Matilda took out a small notebook, and tore a page from it, handing it to Rollison and smiling again. 'That's the man,' she said. 'And I paid enough for that case of salmon heaven knows. It cost thirty-five pounds.'

Soon afterwards Lady Gloria limped and Rollison walked out of the room, Rollison very thoughtful. He knew a chemist who would examine some of the other tins and be discreet, and his first need was to get the case and to send samples for analysis.

When Glory led him to the store-room where the salmon and other things were kept under lock and key he experienced a temporary revulsion of feeling. The store-room was an offence to anti-hoarding laws, morals, and ordinary war-time patriotism.

He was jerked out of a reverie by Lady Gloria.

11

'*Now* I suppose you're going to let her down. If you do I won't forgive you.'

CHAPTER TWO

THE TOFF GOES TO MARKET

Rollison eyed Lady Gloria without expression.

'No,' he said, 'I won't let her down, but I don't feel as sorry for her as I did ten minutes ago. Did you know about this before?'

'I did not.'

'I suppose Patton knows about it?'

'He's the only servant who does, Mattie tells me.'

'That's a help. I'll send Jolly over to collect the case later, so I'd better have the key.' He took it from the lock after turning it.

He looked into the drawing-room again. All but four of the relatives had gone. He did not stay long after seeing Glory safely to her chair, and was glad to step out into the early evening sunlight. Passing the end of Braddon Place was a taxi, and he was at 55 Gresham Terrace ten minutes later.

He saw a curtain move in the window of his flat, and was not surprised to find the front door open and Jolly on the threshold.

Jolly, his man, was the prototype 'gentleman's gentleman', or so Rollison told him in lighter moments. He had other

12

qualifications; he could hold his tongue, use his wits, and—a recent development—he shared Rollison's enthusiasm for quashing crime when opportunity presented.

A man of medium height, Jolly's expression in normal times was one almost of melancholy. His face was lined, his skin was puckered beneath his neck, suggesting that he had once been much fatter but had shrivelled. In the many years that he had worked for Rollison his appearance had not altered except that he was a little greyer at the temples. The Toff did not know his age; he did know that Jolly suffered from dyspepsia, and that his reason for so belying his name in his facial expression was genuine.

Jolly was smiling.

'Good evening, sir. I was delighted to hear that you would be home for a day or two.'

'A few days, I hope,' smiled Rollison, resting a hand on Jolly's shoulder. 'But before we talk about that, I've a job for you.' He took out the key of the cupboard at 7 Braddon Place and placed it in Jolly's hand. 'There is a case of tinned salmon in a cupboard at Lady Matilda's house. Patton knows which it is. Get it and take it to Mr Nevett. Ask him to select a dozen tins at random and to let me have an analysis as soon as he possibly can.'

'Very good, sir,' said Jolly, and added: 'I've prepared a tea-tray, in case you have missed tea, but I am afraid there is nothing in for an

13

evening meal. I thought perhaps you would prefer to go out.'

'All I need for the moment is tea,' said Rollison, and chuckled. 'No over-stocked larder here, Jolly?'

'I have a reasonable store for emergency, sir,' Jolly assured him with dignity.

He went to his room, donned a bowler hat and collected an umbrella, despite the clear blue of the sky and the fact that there had been little rain for several weeks. The back door closed behind him, after he had switched on the electric kettle.

Rollison brewed tea and took it into the living-room.

There was bread-and-butter, biscuits, and a jam sandwich. He leaned back as he ate and drank, and not until he had finished did he take out the slip of paper that Matilda had given him, and read the name and address. In his aunt's handwriting, which had many elegant flourishes, he read:

MR. EDWARD LETT,
41 Gt. Ashley Street, S.W.1.

He finished his tea and went out again, this time travelling by bus to Victoria. He toyed with the idea of telephoning the police and asking them for an opinion of Mr Edward Lett, but decided against it. If he asked for police co-operation he needed a better and more

14

comprehensive story than he could yet offer.

He inquired for Gt. Ashley Street and was directed to walk to the end of Buckingham Palace Gate, and turn right; he would find it either the first or second turning to the left.

He turned into the street at a slow pace, for it was over warm; August had dropped a sultry blanket of hot air on London. Then he saw a thick-set man strolling along one side of the road.

Rollison was not one to speak disparagingly of the police; he held them in great respect, although there were times when in conversation with one or another Yard official he created a different impression. There were a host of Scotland Yard men whom no one would suspect of being detective officers until they chose to disclose their identity, but he knew this to be the stocky figure of Detective-Sergeant 'Happy' Melsom.

He slacked his pace until Melsom reached the far end of the street and then turned.

Rollison needed no more telling that he was watching one of the houses. It was not a careful survey; Melsom, a good man, was advertising his presence, and would only do that deliberately.

Rollison walked more quickly as Melsom approached him.

The stocky man's face was broad and friendly, and had often misled unsuspecting witnesses into believing that Melsom was

15

easily deceived. No more than thirty, he was ear-marked for promotion.

He stopped abruptly.

Rollison smiled, and the detective responded, although warily.

'I didn't expect to see *you*, Mr Rollison.'

'I don't know that I expected to meet you,' admitted Rollison. 'Watching some of the bad men?'

'Watching one of them,' the detective-sergeant admitted.

'And incidentally scaring the life out of him,' rejoined Rollison. 'He wouldn't live at Number Forty-one, would he?'

'So you're after him, too, are you?' said Melsom grimly. There was no doubt that he considered he had scored a point. Rollison proffered cigarettes and glanced across the road; Number 41 was nearly opposite.

'"After him" is an exaggeration,' he said as he struck a match. 'Just interested in him, Happy.'

'I know you and your interest!' exclaimed Melsom. As he drew on his cigarette, his eyes narrowed. 'I think the door's opening. Would you mind...'

He pushed past Rollison, who continued his stroll towards the end of Gt. Ashley Street, wondering whether he could leave the future of Edward Lett safely to the police. He had no particular desire to precipitate himself into action against Lett or any other black

16

marketeers. He felt some reason to hope that the job was already being done when he turned at the corner and saw Melsom walking in the wake of a tall, thin man in grey flannels.

The affair could easily have ended there, although his interest deepened when he returned to the flat to find Jolly already back with a report.

The chemist, Nevett, had examined six tins of the salmon; all of them were tainted; anyone who ate from them would get acute ptomaine poisoning, except the small minority of people whose stomachs were apparently proof against food toxins.

Jolly wondered whether he should open some tins which were not suspect, and prepare a meal.

'The prospect doesn't attract me after that report,' said Rollison. 'I'll have a snack out, Jolly, and go along to see some of the boys. How are they?'

'There is little to report, sir,' said Jolly, who kept a finger on the pulse of the East End, which was the Toff's especial regard. 'Mr Higson asked me today if it was right that you were in town, sir, and Meg Knapp was also interested. I think by this evening they'll all know that you're in London.'

'But there's nothing worth comment?' insisted Rollison.

'Things are very quiet, sir. I was speaking to Superintendent Grice only two days ago; we met quite fortuitously in a restaurant. He assured me that things were quiet, except, of course...' Jolly paused.

'Why and what "of course"?'

'The black market, sir,' said Jolly with some diffidence. 'A great deal of food is being sold outside of rationing. And other things, particularly clothes, wines and spirits, and tobacco. There is an increasing number of prosecutions, and I think the Superintendent was reasonably satisfied with the result of an intensive campaign against the market.'

Rollison frowned.

'Only reasonably satisfied, Jolly?'

'Like yourself, sir, it would take a great deal to fully satisfy Mr Grice.'

Rollison agreed thoughtfully and went out.

It was a little after eight o'clock, and there would be another hour and a half of daylight. He preferred London by day, and had done so even before the black-out. He toyed with the idea of going to the East End before eating, then changed his mind, for his friends there would undoubtedly raid their own larders to make a gargantuan feast when they could ill spare the food.

He went, therefore, to the Regal Hotel.

At the Regal, especially before the war, he had been a frequent, respected, even an honoured guest. He received priority consideration down from Alphonse, the head waiter, through to the *chef*, the older hands

18

amongst the waiters, and the commissionaires. Livy, the Italian wine-steward, whom war regulations had not yet affected, had been known to declare that of his regular patrons only Rollison and seven others were really worthy of the best from the cellar.

Alphonse greeted him, immensely concerned. It was a poor night, but he could recommend a clear soup, grilled sole, and perhaps a savoury to follow. Livy, hovering in the background, was delighted to see Mr Rollison, and ignored the considerable gathering in the dining-room which was crowded with men and women, most of the men in uniform.

There was a surprising lack of filled glasses and bottles. Livy deplored the position, but it was almost impossible to obtain this and that. Nevertheless, for Mr Rollison he could find a little gin, with a really excellent 1929 Niersteiner with the fish. Yes?

'Thanks, Livy,' smiled Rollison. 'I'll be satisfied with the Niersteiner.'

'You are as thoughtful as ever, signor. I live to hope that you will see the return of better days. Signor, if you were to visit my cellar...' Livy raised his hands in a positively Gallic gesture. 'It desolates me! Bin after bin, quite empty. *Quite* empty, but for dust and cobwebs.'

'I suppose we have to expect wine to run short,' said Rollison, seeing a dozen eyes

19

turned towards him.

'Expect, yes,' said Livy, and then in a lower voice: 'It can be obtained, signor, but at a price—what a price! I am happy to say that I am not permitted to buy except through the regular merchants, but at times I wonder, is that wise?'

'So there *is* plenty about,' said Rollison slowly.

'It is what you call corned, signor. No, excuse me, cornered! You will perhaps recall that there was to be a sale of Milord Tantham's cellar. I was to be there,' Livy added, and his long, thin face with the hot brown eyes grew animated. 'What a day it was to be! But the sale was withdrawn, you will remember. Afterwards I heard why. Much was to be sold at prices which were absurd; dealers they called themselves—it is enough to make a good judge of wines ill. Dealers! With their big cheques and their fat profits! Why is not more done about such roguery?'

'Why indeed,' echoed Rollison.

'But I am absurd to worry Signor Rollison with such talk,' declared Livy. 'Also I perceive that I am wanted.' He turned, and saw a big, red-faced man beckoning him. Rollison watched his face, and was amused at the blank expression which suddenly descended on it.

Aunt Matilda and Jolly had given him much to think about on the activities of the black market. Livy had added enough to make him
20

really curious and to feel the first niggling of an awareness that he would like to do something about it. He finished a meal which was excellent within wartime limits, and left the Regal.

He went by bus to Aldgate.

In the proper mood Rollison would say that he suffered, or experienced, a peculiar metamorphosis whenever he left the City and entered Aldgate. In an expansive moment he would even say that this transformation had first descended upon him in his youth, when for the first time he had visited Petticoat Lane on a Sunday morning.

Hitherto Petticoat Lane had been a thing to hear about and marvel at; but the two things which stuck most in his memory of that first visit were (a) the astonishing change from the deserted streets of the City, with their grey, gaunt buildings and the ghostly silence of the Sabbath to the throngs in Aldgate High Street and the eager crowds in Petticoat Lane itself, and (b) a disappointment at discovering that Petticoat Lane was actually the much mundane Middlesex Street.

The disappointment faded into fascination of deserted streets which suddenly turned into crowded roads and pavements; of silent banks and business houses to the stridency of the street stalls and shouting proprietors and touts outside an amazing miscellany of shops. All of this lingered and remained indelible. He sometimes thought that his first visit here had seen the birth of his interest in the East End.

To many it was just a crowd of Jews and East-Enders with a sprinkling of lascars and Chinese, and some well-dressed sightseers often with their noses high in the air. To him it was a kaleidoscopic spectacle of a teeming mass of eager humanity bartering and bantering, all astonishingly good-humoured, from the fruit-stall hawkers to the sellers of gherkins and other oily foods. There was everywhere a hint of the bazaars of the Orient and the Oriental love of bargaining and haggling.

Since that first visit he had grown into a man who was known, respected, liked and perhaps above all feared, in the East End. There he had been dubbed 'the Toff' because in a whimisical mood he had strolled through the streets wearing a top hat and a monocle, morning suit and a swagger cane. From the moment he appeared in Aldgate in those clothes rumours of his arrival had spread fast; within a few hours the whole of the district had known that the Toff was in London.

Very soon the rumours spread with equal facility whether he was in morning dress, a lounge suit or in uniform. Many hated his appearance although the majority welcomed him, for he had done much to bring about a better understanding between the 'natives' and the police.

On that warm evening he walked along Aldgate High Street for a few minutes, receiving a hundred nods and smiles and eventually reached the 'Lion', a tavern owned by a firm of brewers and tenanted by one Sammy Diver.

There were gaps in the houses on either side, and just off the High Street was a monumental pile of rubble, one of Hitler's paw-marks still nakedly evident in the East End. The people had grown used to the sight, and for a long time they had been immune from bombing.

Rollison went into the saloon bar, and half a dozen people looked towards him. The effect was not unlike that of his entry at 7 Braddon Place—except that after the first hushed moment there was a torrent of exclamation, of greeting, of offers to buy him drinks.

Behind the bar was a little red-nosed man, earning his nickname of Sniffy, and a monstrous woman with flaming cheeks and a vast mop of dark hair, hot brown eyes—not unlike Livy's; Rollison knew there was Italian blood in her ancestry—and a vast bosom restrained by a taut silk dress.

Her features were broad and coarse, but there was a beauty of line in them which many an artist wanted to paint. She had been an artist's model and lived a strange life until Sammy Diver had met and married her; the freak union was the more freakish because the marriage of the thin-faced little Cockney to the full-blooded Eliza had flourished and prospered and proved happy.

Rollison always waited for a moment before she spoke, preparing for the shock to come. She was a magnificent creature, in appearance no more than a decade away from her ancestors' Tuscany; and she talked broad Cockney.

A path was made for Rollison, who imagined a faint atmosphere of restraint despite the boisterousness of their greeting and wondered what caused it. The red-nosed man was the barman; Sammy Diver was not in sight.

'Hallo, Liz,' Rollison said as he reached the bar. 'Aren't you rich enough to retire yet?'

'Watcher, me old cocksparrer. 'Ow are yer?' She extended a work-grained hand and Rollison took it firmly. 'Strewth, I never expected to see yer, strike me!'

'I didn't expect myself,' said Rollison for the second time that day. 'Where's Sammy?'

The hot eyes smouldered as she stared at him, and he was puzzled by the curtness of her reply.

'Hupstairs. 'E's ill. Watcher goin' to 'ave?'

'Beer, please,' said the Toff.

'In a tank an' on the 'ouse,' declared Lizzie, and looked past the Toff.

He drank her health, and then glanced behind him. There were a dozen unfamiliar faces, as many friendly ones, but only one

24

which was staring towards him coldly and without expression. It was a thin, regular face, apparently of a man who took life sombrely. He was dressed in black, which emphasized the pallor of his face.

The man turned to a neighbour and began to speak, while Rollison exchanged greetings with the several men who pushed their way towards him. Variously he was described as 'Mr Ar', 'the Torf' and 'Mr Rawlison'. The atmosphere of restraint eased, but he believed it remained, fancied that Lizzie's cryptic *''e's ill'* had been dictated by something he did not properly comprehend.

The man in black was talking in undertones to a bowler-hatted man who had one cauliflower ear when the conversation was interrupted when the door opened with a heavy bang. A hefty man entered, commanding attention with a loud:

'I've gotta n'earful!'

He paused. His ugly face was animated and he was not the type to make the announcement without being able to prove it. There were one or two 'Okay, let's 'ave its'.

''Appy Melsom's got 'is. They just pulled 'im out've the river. That'll mean trouble, that will. You don't git a dick rubbed out for nuthink. Liz, I don't arf want a wet, make it snappy.'

He pushed his way towards the bar while Rollison was repeating the words to himself; or those of them that really mattered.

"'Appy Melsom's got 'is; they just pulled 'im out've the river.'

Rollison assimilated the bald announcement as the bringer of bad tidings reached the bar. The room buzzed with excited comment. Melsom had been a popular officer, as Yard men went; he would have been proud of the coarse-tongued obituary.

It was then that the man in black left the 'Lion'.

Rollison, noting the expressionless face, fancied there was a gleam of satisfaction in his eyes before he turned away. It entered Rollison's mind to follow the man, but he dismissed it as an unreasonable impulse and turned to ask for details of Melsom's death.

Afterwards he believed he had made a mistake by following reason instead of instinct.

CHAPTER THREE

WARNING FOR THE TOFF

The husky man was named Harry, he was a stevedore at the Wapping docks, and had been on duty when Melsom's body had been pulled out of the river by a lighter-man who had lost no time in identifying him and little in sending for the River Police. Melsom had been killed with a knife, stabbed in the chest before being thrown into the river.

Towards the end of the narrative, the saloon bar hummed with talk. Harry was sullen when he realized that he no longer held the spotlight, and drank in silence. Rollison ordered another beer, and his tankard was being refilled when there was a tug at his coat. He looked round and down as a diminutive little man peered up into his face, jerking his head towards a corner.

Lizzie was busy; what was more remarkable, she was too busy to talk to the Toff, who had always been welcome at the 'Lion'. It was not imagination, thought Rollison, that she was nervous of him.

And her husband was 'ill'.

The sensation of Melsom's murder had taken the spotlight from the Toff also. Harry cheered up when others entered and wanted fresh details, while Rollison joined the little man in a corner where there were two vacant chairs.

He knew the other, who was not a dwarf, nor misshapen; he was simply a little man.

'Now what's worrying you, Joe?'

'Me, I ain't worried,' said Joe, screwing up his leathery face and then hiding it in a glass. 'Not me, I ain't worried. Thought I'd give yer a word in time, that's all. I ain't one to let a friend dahn; you know me.'

'I know you,' agreed Rollison.

'Thought you'd like ter know,' went on Joe,

a delinquent who often found himself at one or other of the Metropolitan police courts, usually on a charge of being drunk and disorderly. 'That bloke; strewth, give me the shivers 'e did. The cove in black, did yer see 'im? 'E come in just after you.'

Rollison nodded.

'Wanted ter know who you was,' continued Joe, and paused again to hide his face. 'Beer!' he exclaimed, as he lowered the glass. 'It ain't beer, it's coloured water. 'Strewth, the brewers mustn't arf be makin' a profit!' He stared at Rollison, and there was warning in his little eyes. 'Wanted to know who yer was, 'e did. I 'eard 'im askin'. Perce, the silly bastid, told 'im you was the Torf. Some coves can't keep their mouth shut, never could and never can. I just thought I'd tell yer.'

'Thanks, Joe,' said Rollison appreciatively. 'Who is the man in black?'

'Dunno, Mr Ar.'

'Do you see much of him?'

'Comes in now and again. Seen 'im before. Like a blinkin' undertaker, that's wot I says. Look of 'im gives yer the shivers, don't it? I'll tell yer wot, Mr Ar, just in case you gits curious like. I seen 'im with Perky Lowe—remember 'im? Useter pass a lot o' snide, but he's grown out've it; no one would take 'is money.'

'Thanks,' said Rollison. It might be useful later on. 'What will you have?'

'No more for me, ta. 'Ad me ration.
28

Goo'night, Mr Ar. Watch yerself.'

Joe heaved himself from his chair and made his way to the door with speed and agility, less than shoulder-high to every man he passed.

The bar was crowded by then, the smoke was thick. Harry's voice could be heard declaiming to newcomers the full details of finding Melsom. Lizzie was hot and flustered behind the bar. She deliberately avoided Rollison's eyes when he looked her way.

He found no difficulty in getting to the bar again, and he made Lizzie take notice of him at last. She spoke with a bluster which failed to conceal the fact that she was ill at ease.

'Another, Mr Ar? Ain't forgotten 'ow to put it down then, ha-ha-ha!' She tossed back her dark mane of hair and her laugh was a bellow. 'Nice to see yer lookin' so well!'

'I'd like to see Sammy,' said Rollison.

Her lips tightened. She drew his beer and put it in front of him, while two people spoke to him at the same time.

'Sorry, Mr Ar. Doc's orders, 'e's seein' no one. Glad to oblige, otherwise. Big 'Arry, yer can't stay in my 'ouse an' talk yer 'ead orf without drinkin'; what's it to be?' She gave her attention to the loquacious Harry, getting a laugh at his expense. Rollison turned, but was blocked by men who wanted to yarn with him.

He reached the street at last.

Inside the heat had been stifling; outside it was better only because there was no odour of

29

beer and tobacco.

His wrist-watch told him it was ten minutes to ten.

There were many other places in the East End where he could have obtained information, yet he felt an urge to see the police. He could telephone them, but doubted whether that would serve his purpose as well as a visit to the Yard. The Yard would be handling the inquiry into Melsom's death as a matter of urgency.

There was a taxi near the station. He got in, and said:

'Scotland Yard.'

Over the western sky there loomed a dark cloud which made the twilight fade swiftly, and by the time he was in Whitehall it was pitch dark except for the dull glow of shelter signs, bright car-lights, and the torches of pedestrians. In the cab he had some relief from the sweltering heat because of a draught, but as soon as he was on the pavement in Little Parliament Street, the heat closed about him again.

'How much?' he asked.

'Two an' six, please.'

He was feeling for the coins in his pocket when he heard the first rush of feet. He turned, more curious than alarmed; and then a dark shape launched itself at him.

A fist was aimed wildly at his head; the blow missed, although Rollison felt the wind of it.

Suddenly he was in the centre of a milling crowd, and he felt the heavy weight of a cosh on his shoulder. Something struck the peak of his hat and forced it down to his nose. There was heavy breathing about him, an occasional oath; he was crowded against the cab.

Then someone hissed: ''Op in!'

It was the taxi-driver.

Rollison was vaguely aware that the man was leaning backwards from his seat with the door of the cab wide open. For a split second he wondered whether he was wise to entrust himself to the cabby, but there were at least half a dozen men between the shops in Parliament Street and himself. He cracked his fist into the face of a man who ran at him, avoiding a kick to the groin, stepped back on to the running board and got in.

The engine snorted.

A man made a last-minute grab at him, but Rollison was safely inside the cab and facing the pavement. He gripped the man's wrist, tightened the grip and jerked the man towards him. There was a howl of sheer terror, and then a crunching sound; the door, swinging to, had squeezed the man's legs against the running-board.

They had covered perhaps twenty yards when Rollison managed to hold the door open and drag his victim into the cab. The driver turned towards Westminster Bridge and then along the Embankment. There was no sound

31

of pursuit, although the echo of a police whistle blown too late reached Rollison's ears.

The victim had collapsed on the floor of the cab and was moaning and groaning.

The cab stopped, and the driver reached the door and opened it before Rollison had time to move. The glow of a torch shone, and the cabby said tensely:

'I thought that was the best thing, Mr Ar ... Gawd!'

He saw the unknown passenger. In the reflected glow of his torch he gaped.

'We'd better drive right up to the steps,' Rollison said.

'Okay.' The man hurried off, the cab went on again until a policeman stopped it outside the iron gates, and a torch shone into Rollison's face. The invisible constable behind it said:

'Registration card or pass, please. I—oh, Mr Rollison!'

'I'm glad no one's forgotten me,' said Rollison, 'Is Superintendent Grice in?'

'He arrived not ten minutes ago, sir.'

'Good, thanks. Is there room in Cannon Row for this?'

'This what, sir?'

'This man who attacked me,' said Rollison.

The victim had lost consciousness, but Rollison had made sure that his legs were not broken. The trousers were torn, and the right leg bared almost to the bone; torchlight had revealed both facts. There had been no time to take a comprehensive look at the other's face before the stop at the Yard.

The constable showed a praiseworthy restraint.

'Probably due for a hospital, not Cannon Row, sir.'

'More than likely,' admitted Rollison. 'But don't let him get away. The Superintendent will want to ask him a lot of questions. If you're worried about formalities, I'll charge him with common assault.'

'That's all right, sir.'

Other policemen arrived, torches converged on the injured man, and Rollison left him.

He took a pound note from his wallet and handed it to the cabby.

'And that doesn't begin to tell you how grateful I am,' he said. 'When did you recognize me?'

'At Aldgit, sir. Thank *you.*'

'Do you live in Aldgate?'

'No, sir, Bethnel Green. I never knew you was being followed, but now I comes to think of it there was 'arf a dozen blokes 'anging around, just behind you. You wants to watch your step, Mr Ar; we can't do wivvout you.'

'I hope you won't need to,' said Rollison. 'What's your name?'

'Myers, sir. 18 Lea Lane, but if you don't mind I'd rather not have to give evidence—if you see what I mean.'

'I do indeed,' said Rollison. 'Thanks again, Myers. Don't talk about this, will you?'

'I'm a clam,' announced Myers, and let in the clutch.

It was half an hour after he had first left the cab and been attacked when Rollison walked slowly up the steps of Scotland Yard, his head still buzzing. He did not try to think until he was sitting in the hall of the Yard and a sergeant was telephoning Superintendent Grice. The heat was now almost unbearable, as much due to his exertion as to the humidity. He dabbed at his forehead, when the sergeant replaced the receiver and said:

'He'll be glad to see you, sir. Do you know his office?'

'Yes, thanks,' said Rollison.

The Yard was well blacked-out, and consequently well lighted. He walked briskly along the stone corridors, up one flight of stairs, and then tapped at a green-painted door. A precise voice, very clear, invited him in.

When Rollison had first met Superintendent Grice he had thought the man no more like a policeman than Lady Gloria was. Second, third, and fourth impressions had not revised the first estimate. Grice might have been taken anywhere for an ascetic. He was thin, his features were not handsome but very clear-cut, the skin stretched tightly over his high-bridged nose. His brown hair was slightly over-long and he had light brown eyes which could look baleful, thin lips well-shaped.

Grice had been among the many policemen who had started new on work in the East End who had scoffed at the Toff and then suspected him of collaboration with the more criminal-minded elements of the area east of Aldgate Pump. He had taken considerable persuading to the contrary, but, once converted, had made a complete *volte face*.

He was alone in the large office, standing up and approaching the door as Rollison entered. They shook hands, and Grice smiled enough to show very white teeth. He was dressed in brown, even to his tie.

'I'm glad to see you, Rollison; I'd no idea you were in town. Sit down.' He pushed up a green-leather upholstered chair, passed a box of cigarettes, and stood for a moment looking down at the Toff. His smile faded as Rollison took a cigarette—Grice himself rarely smoked.

'Have you had a rough-and-tumble?'

'That's it,' admitted Rollison. 'I'm damned if I know where to begin.'

'It's been an unusual night altogether,' said Grice slowly. 'And this caps it.' He dabbed his forehead, for the office was baking hot.

'I think I'll smoke for five minutes and put my thoughts in order,' Rollison said. 'I've had some greetings at the Yard, but this was the warmest.'

He smiled a little at Grice's sharp change of

expression, but the telephone rang and he had a few minutes to think while Grice discussed the murder of Melsom.

Grice finished, and sat back in a swivelchair. There was a large pedestal desk between them, immaculate and shiny.

'Feeling better?' he asked.

'Almost myself,' said Rollison. 'It all started from a rumour about a Mr Edward Lett.' He ignored the narrowing of Grice's eyes, and, omitting only the truth about his indirect introduction to Lett, told the full story, including a *resume* of his conversation with Jolly.

Finally, he said:

'I haven't tried to sort it out yet, but I would say that I was seen talking to Melsom, and recognized by the man in black at the "Lion." The more I think of it the more I think that's likely. I suspect that he decided that I was taking too much interest in Lett, and read into my trip to the "Lion" an ulterior motive. So I was followed from Aldgate and according to plan I should have been beaten up. Not nice people; they don't even declare war.'

'We've declared it on them,' said Grice grimly. 'Melsom was watching Lett. We hoped to scare Lett into a false move. I think we have,' he added. 'He's under arrest, and on the way here now. We've known for some time that he's been selling on the black market, but—'

'I don't think I can stand the next comment,'

murmured Rollison. 'You're going to tell me he's an agent, a pawn, a tool, a puppet, a cat's-paw. Of course he might be the kingpin,' he ended hopefully.

Grice shook his head.

'Lett doesn't count for much, but I must question him in the hope of getting a lead on Melsom's murderer. Melsom certainly followed him. He left a report with a patrolman in Aldgate, then went towards the river. Lett was ahead of him then, and we picked Lett up near Epping.'

'You don't think there's much chance of getting what you want to know from him?'

'I'm going to be pleasantly surprised if he knows anything of significance,' said Grice. 'Rollison, the scope and extent of buying on the black market is increasing much too fast. I think one of the centres is in the East End. I've been seriously considering getting in touch with you—you can help more down there than any man living. If we can persuade the War Office to grant you leave, will you drop everything and work in with us?'

CHAPTER FOUR

GRICE TELLS A STORY

Rollison rubbed the side of his chin slowly. He knew that the Superintendent would normally resist any temptation to ask directly for help. The effort it must have cost Grice made Rollison realize for the first time that the black marketing must have reached a dangerous high level.

Of course it had; he should have sensed it.

The prices were far too high for the Regal; that was indication enough that it was beyond the ordinary under-cover dealing.

He thought of Lizzie, and her fear that she should be seen talking to him too freely; for fear it had been. He did not doubt that he had been attacked because (a) he had talked to Melsom and (b) he had visited the 'Lion'. So presumably he could have obtained information from Lizzie.

Grice picked up a pen and eyed it closely.

'There are moments when I would give a lot to know just what you're thinking,' he remarked.

'Just then I was thinking of my C.O. and his likely reaction,' Rollison said mendaciously. 'I don't know that I'd like to have an official connection. Rumours spread. Once it gets round that I'm working with the police what influence I have would be gone in a couple of puffs.'

'I was afraid you'd feel like that,' admitted Grice.

'Why afraid? I can be much more use as a freelance. I'll see the C.O. in the morning,' Rollison added, 'and put it to him. Meanwhile if you'd care to unburden yourself—'

'I'll check on the man you've brought in, and then give you an outline,' said Grice. He pulled the telephone towards him and gave instructions for a report to be telephoned about the cab victim.

He had replaced the receiver and was arranging the papers on his desk neatly, when the door opened and abruptly to admit a man who entered without ceremony and said:

'Grice, is this true about Melsom?'

Grice stood up slowly. Rollison smiled up at the newcomer amiably, but was ignored and perhaps unnoticed by the Hon. Humphrey Stoddart, Assistant Commissioner at Scotland Yard.

'I'm afraid it is, sir,' Grice said.

Stoddart unwound a silk scarf from his neck, an unexpected thing because of the heat. He tossed it on a chair, then appeared to notice Rollison. He paused; and his broad, large-featured face showed surprise but also a hint of gratification.

'Hal-*lo*, Rollison! Are you in this?'

'I tried the water with my toes and Grice is trying to take me for a cross-channel swim,' said Rollison.

'I hope he succeeds,' said Stoddart.

Grice gave him particulars, as far as they were available, of Melsom's murder. There was nothing new to the Toff, except that the story was put in more formal phraseology. Big Harry's account was repeated. Grice added that Edward Lett was on the way to the Yard, and that Rollison had seen Melsom in Gt. Ashley Street.

Stoddart eyed Rollison with his head on one side. He was a big man, not particularly tall but powerful and lithe-moving.

'I thought you'd only put your toes in?'

'Metaphorically speaking,' murmured the Toff.

'He doesn't get any better, does he?' said Stoddart. 'Come along to my room; we'll be more comfortable there, and you can tell Rollison the whole story. I need a refresher myself,' he added, and for Rollison's benefit: 'I've had a few days off. Touch of malaria.'

Rollison understood Stoddart's scarf then.

They went to the A.C.'s office on the same floor. Stoddart's bushy grey eyebrows gave him an air of fierce expectancy; his broad, bulky figure made even casual movements seem aggressive.

The easy chairs in the room were large and comfortable, and the room was cooler.

'It's been going on in a small way for two years, of course,' Grice began. 'From the moment some commodities grew scarce someone cornered the market. We were too busy to give it much attention, and it got a firmer hold than any of us liked. Then when food was rationed and grew short, the black market widened its scope. The Ministry of Food kept tightening the screw, but not enough. Even with much heavier fines and the prison sentences there is a great amount of what we term the "ordinary" buying and selling.'

Stoddart nodded.

'But every now and again some little thing has happened to make us realize that it's on a much bigger scale than we suspected,' went on Grice. 'From time to time van-loads of food have disappeared, with other rationed commodities—far more than you would realize by studying the Press. You probably remember that some time ago there was a big-scale effort to sabotage our food?' He paused only just long enough for Rollison to nod, and continued; 'That was sabotage on a grand scale, and black-marketing with a scope hitherto not conceived. The Secret Intelligence handled it, with the Special Branch. We weren't directly concerned, because at the time the food wasn't put back on the market. Now food is being put back—food, clothes, wines, spirits, anything you like to think of that's in

41

short supply. There are thousands of completely British "citizens"'—Grice sneered that word, while Rollison thought of Aunt Matilda—'who will pay anything for whatever they can get. We've caught some of them. They don't hesitate to pay five hundred per cent of the retail value of the goods; they even seem to like it.'

Grice leaned forward and picked up a pen. He was sitting opposite Stoddart, with Rollison at one end of a large, flat-topped desk. Stoddart and Rollison were smoking, and Stoddart leaned down and opened a drawer in the desk, motioning Grice to go on. Grice's next words were accompanied by the tinkle of glasses, and once by a *thump*! as a bottle fell to the carpet.

'No harm done,' grunted Stoddart.

Grice was saying:

'We discovered that Lett was selling to a wide circle of customers some three months ago, and we went to see him and gave him a warning. Then we let him go, believing that he would have to keep contact with his suppliers, or employers, and that he would lead us to them. But he's always avoided taking us to the fountain-head. We've made several arrests and commandeered a host of supplies, but all the time we have a damnably uncomfortable feeling that someone is sitting back and laughing at us.'

Stoddart poured two whiskies, and pushed

one to Rollison, with a soda-syphon.

'Thanks,' said Rollison, and squirted soda liberally.

Grice paused long enough to sip a lemon and tonic, and then spoke in a grimmer voice.

'That's a brief outline of the situation, Rolly. We know there are large stocks of practically every commodity in short supply, up and down the country. Occasionally they flood the market. I'm inclined to wonder whether there aren't two organizations, working against each other. But there's another and much more worrying angle—I nearly said "more serious", and in some ways it is. When buyers are reluctant, or when a shopkeeper or innkeeper won't touch the black market—and there are plenty of them—they're deliberately attacked. As you were tonight. We haven't made anyone admit it yet, but the general impression among my men is that it's a protection racket of the worst kind. It applies particularly to public houses, but there have been other instances. You won't need telling that we can't let it go any further.'

He finished, pedantic to the last, and took a deeper drink.

Stoddart smiled.

'A master of understatement, isn't he, Rollison? The Home Office and Ministry of Food are running neck-and-neck in telling us it's got to stop. That's how bad it is.'

Rollison pushed his chair back, stood up,

and lit another cigarette.

'So we're high up in the air,' he said. 'No contact apart from Lett, my man in black, and the little beggar I grabbed tonight. Blackie is an indirect contact, so that leaves us fifty-fifty.' He flicked a flame from his lighter, and murmured that he would not object to another whisky-and-soda. Stoddart obliged, and Rollison went on thoughtfully: 'Outside of Lett, you've no one else?'

'No one who's not in jail,' said Stoddart.

'And the golden rule is silence,' mused the Toff. 'A queer kind of loyalty, but no honour among thieves; that shibboleth was exploded long ago. They're being bribed to keep silent, of course. Before they get caught there's always a *cache* set aside for them to collect when they come out, and all convictions so far have earned short sentences. Short, that is, for old-timers. If Lett were worried about a murder charge he might talk.'

'Knowing Lett, I don't think so,' said Grice.

'I was told of a man named Perky Lowe tonight,' Rollison said. 'I remember him vaguely; he worked a racecourse racket and operated a gang. Has he appeared in this?'

'I know Lowe,' said Grice, 'but not in this connection.'

'I'll look him up,' promised Rollison.

As he finished the telephone rang. Stoddart answered it, then pushed it across to Grice.

'Yes,' said Grice into the mouthpiece. 'Yes

44

... I see. Get all you can about him and his friends, Anderson. Is Lett here yet? ... All right, give me a ring as soon as he arrives.' He replaced the telephone and looked hard at Rollison.

'The man you caught,' Grice announced slowly, 'is Perky Lowe. He says he was walking along Whitehall when half a dozen men suddenly ran at a taxi, and he got in the way. It's not a bad argument.'

'Not bad at all,' agreed Stoddart. 'We aren't dealing with fools.'

'We'll find out what we can about Lowe's gang,' said Grice crisply, 'and we'll hold him for some time. He might get worried.'

'Do you know,' said Rollison thoughtfully, 'I wouldn't hold him, I would let him go. He can be watched—in fact I'd like to watch him myself.'

'Hmm,' said Stoddart.

'Please yourselves,' said Rollison with a shrug. 'Which leads us to a point of some importance.' He regarded both Stoddart and Grice with one eyebrow raised slightly above the other. 'If I can come into this, on what basis do I work?'

'On what basis will you want to work?' Stoddart demanded.

'Reasonable freedom of movement, and an understanding that if I think it's wiser not to report progress I don't.'

'I see,' said Stoddart. 'You want to play us

45

for flatfoots, and go your own sweet way.'
Rollison imagined that Grice was looking at
his A.C. appealingly. Stoddart had far less
humour than Grice, was much more cut-and-
dried in his ideas and conceptions. The
principle was the thing with Stoddart; Grice
worked only for results.

Stoddart shrugged at last.

'Don't go getting yourself into trouble,' he
said.

'It will be useful if we know you're working
with us,' Grice said.

'As soon as I've seen the C.O. I'll phone
you,' promised Rollison. 'And now it's getting
late; I want to be a bright-eyed sleuth in the
morning.'

'Aren't you going to wait to see Lett?'

'You see Lett,' said Rollison. 'You can ask
questions much more effectively. I should
probably want to make him punch-drunk first.
There is one thing—the man dubbed Blackie.
Has he shown up anywhere else?'

'Your description doesn't ring any bell,'
admitted Grice.

'You're getting much too figurative in
speech,' chided Rollison. 'I've always thought
of you as the Yard's one pedant, but what with
"rackets" and "ringing the bell", you're
slipping. Seriously, now'—in that moment he
looked almost sombre, and both men eyed
him—'I'll get into it with both feet as fast as I
can.'

He left the office after cordial good nights, and was as cordially treated by the several uniformed men he saw on the way to the front entrance. It was pitch dark outside, and a constable lighted the steps as he walked down. He stood for some seconds once the torch was switched off, to accustom his eyes to the darkness.

There was much on his mind, but it weighed lightly compared with the possibility that someone would be waiting for him to leave the Yard. He was half-prepared for a second assault, but reached the point some way along Whitehall safely.

'I'm getting too imaginative,' he rebuked himself. 'What shall I do—get a cab or walk?'

He decided to walk.

It remained sultry and oppressive, but the storm held off, and he saw some patches of clear sky in which stars winked down at him. London's buildings rose on either side, shadowy giants frowning down. Once or twice a bus lumbered past, but there was little traffic. From behind him Big Ben sent a sonorous note, its peal telling him that it was a quarter to one.

If the walk did not refresh him, it made his mind clearer. He was in a much easier frame of mind when he reached the flat. He did not think Jolly would have gone to bed and was looking forward to talking to him.

His flat was on the top floor. The front door

47

of the house was open, since there were five flats in all, and the main entrance was a communal one, each flat with its own front door. There was carpet to soften footsteps in the hall and the passage, and up the stairs. Rollison had often regretted that, for it allowed visitors who could be unwelcome to approach without giving him due warning.

Yet the carpeting did not muffle the sound of breathing.

Nor did his movements.

He heard it clearly when he reached the stairs. It was ahead of him, a laboured, perhaps stifled breathing. It made him pause, and he put his hand to his holster and, for the first time that day, drew out his Service revolver. The faint sound as he drew it out merged with the breathing, which grew louder as he went cautiously upstairs; it was as if someone in the throes of a great emotion was waiting there.

He reached the landing, and then switched on his torch.

'Oh!' gasped a woman.

She moved a few feet ahead of him, and the light of his torch revealed her massive figure, while her breathing grew tumultuous.

Rollison recovered his composure in time to say:

'Hallo, Lizzie. What brings you?'

CHAPTER FIVE

WHAT HAPPENED TO SAM DIVER

'It—it is you, Mr Ar?'

Lizzie's whisper must have penetrated into the flat, behind the front door of which there was a faint glow. In the torchlight she looked grotesque.

'Yes, of course,' he said. 'Why didn't you wait inside?'

She did not answer, but clutched his arm.

He had been surprised to see her; now he realized that he should have expected the call, for Lizzie believed in him and trusted in him no matter how she acted.

Jolly opened the door.

'Good . . .' and was doubtless going to say 'evening', for any time before bedtime was evening to Jolly. He stopped abruptly, staring at Lizzie, then recovered swiftly.

'Good evening, sir.'

'Make some coffee, Jolly, will you?' Rollison armed Lizzie into the flat, closed the door, and led her across the hall into the living-room.

She was dressed as she had been at the 'Lion', except that she wore a scarlet scarf of silk about her magnificent black hair. She gave the impression that she had made herself up before leaving home, but perspiration had ruined the makeup, while in her eyes was fear; a hot, urgent fear.

'Oh, Mr Ar!' she gasped. 'Oh, Mr Ar, I'm scared o' me own shadow!'

'It's big enough to frighten you,' said Rollison drily, and proffered her a cigarette.

The sally made her lips curve.

'All the best people run to fat,' she retorted, puffing away, 'Ta. Oh, Mr Ar, am I scared!'

'You didn't come here to tell me that,' said Rollison, sitting down when she was in an armchair, which she dwarfed. 'I knew that there was something on your mind—between you and me, I came away from the "Lion" feeling pretty sore at you.'

'I never meant it,' said Lizzie earnestly. 'I never meant to cause no offence, Mr Ar. I just never knew wot I was doing or thinkin'; I don't these days. Me 'ead goes round and round somethink chronic. Mr Ar—no one knows I'm 'ere, do they?'

'No one could,' said Rollison. 'But why didn't you wait inside?'

'I 'adn't been there long,' said Lizzie obscurely.

She went on to tell him that an hour before she had telephoned the flat, to be told by Jolly that he, Mr Rollison, was expected any time. She had hurried from the 'Lion' to Gresham Terrace, and tried to make up her mind to knock. It was easy to see that she found that difficult. Yet in the room, and with the Toff

50

sitting opposite her, she was much more at ease.

Rollison was smiling, a dark-haired, sunburned man with confident and reassuring grey eyes, clear-cut features and a squarish chin with a cleft, a straight nose perhaps a little over-long and a short upper-lip newly clean-shaven.

''Strewth,' said Lizzie, when she had finished, 'Now I feel better!' She gave a wide smile, showing fine, natural teeth, and then Jolly came in. She looked up at him boldly, and laughed. 'Wotcher, Misery, 'ow are yer?'

'Very well, Mrs Diver, thank you.' Jolly had quite recovered his composure.

Lizzie roared; her laughter must have sounded gargantuan in the flat above.

Jolly gravely poured coffee and retired to the kitchen, but did not close the door; he would listen, and hear as much of Lizzie's story as the Toff.

The coffee was hot, and Lizzie grimaced as she took a sip. Her fear may have eased, but she was still on edge.

'Mr Ar,' she said, 'I was afraid to say anything tonight, I never know who's listening these days. That's Gawd's truth, I never know. Listen; I got to tell yer this: Sammy ain't ill. Not *ill*. He was beaten up. Beaten up,' repeated Lizzie, and her massive hands bunched. 'I'd like to slit their gizzards, the b—! D'yer know why it was? I'll tell yer. Just because Sammy's

51

got a conshence, that's wot. A conshence. 'E never would touch the dirty stuff; 'e sells the best an' nothing else, but they 'ad a go at 'im because 'e wouldn't buy their dirty likker.'

Rollison did not interrupt. Lizzie had paused, but was not inviting comment. She was looking into the past and what she hoped would be the brighter future.

'It was like this, Mr Ar. Some man come an' offered Sammy a gross o' whisky. Whisky, real Scotch. 'Strewth, it's harder to get than a tip out of its maker, that's wot it is. But lissen— five pound a bottle, 'e wanted. Five pound! 'E 'ad the ruddy nerve to say Sammy could water it down. Sammy ain't watered a drop o' beer, never mind whisky, in 'is life. My Sammy's a straight one, an' I'll tell the world. 'E turned it down, and then the little runt got nasty. Said 'e'd better change 'is mind, 'e did. So Sammy ups an' tells 'im quick, lemme tell yer 'e didn't waste no time an' no words. Clear out of 'is house, 'e said, or 'e'd fetch the dicks.' She paused, and fixed the Toff with her eyes, blazing then with fervour. 'My Sammy ain't no squealer, yer knows that as well as I do.'

'Sammy's all right,' said the Toff.

'Okay, then Sammy's all right. 'E'd fetch the dicks, 'e would, if the man never cleared out. 'E wasn't no squealer, but sellin' whisky on the black was more than 'e would stand, an' I weighed in an' told that little runt wot I thought of 'im, too. He cleared out, but he said we'd regret it. Regret it!' She threw back her head and laughed, harshly and without humour. 'We never give it another thought, Mr Ar, till the next day. That was when they beat Sammy up. Yer oughta see 'im. It'll take a month for 'im to mend; more'n a month I reckon. They smashed three of 'is ribs, broke 'is nose, an' cut 'is mouth somethink awful. Cor, I wanted to cry. They told 'im he'd get worse if he went to the dicks, see. That's wot did it— that an' because he wouldn't buy their dirty likker.'

She paused looking a little woebegone, almost as if she were ashamed of her outburst.

'Well, there y'are, Mr Ar.' She spoke more quietly. 'I had a doctor in, an' Sammy was put ter bed. We 'ad to 'ave a nurse all the week. The bandages ain't off yet, an' that 'appened a fortnight ago, not a day less.' She paused and put a beringed finger on Rollison's knee. 'An' wot do yer think 'appened next?'

The Toff hardly needed to think, but did not spoil Lizzie's story.

'I don't know,' he said gravely.

'I'll tell yer. The very next day the man comes again. The *same* ruddy li'l tike comes again, an' offered me the gross at *six pun'* a bottle. Six *pun'*! But—wot could I do, Mr Ar? I'm only a woman, even if I am outsize, an' I 'ad to carry on the 'ouse, didn't I? It wasn't no use goin' to the dicks. So I paid up. I bought two more lots since then, at the same price. It's

53

ruinin' us, Mr Ar, an' I ain't 'ad the 'eart to tell Sammy yet.'

'What did Sam say when he came round?'

'He just said wait until 'e was all right again, he'd give Lowe more'n 'e expected.'

'Who?' Rollison spoke sharply.

'Why, Perky Lowe; it was his gang wot did it. They don't do so much racin' these days, an' Percy loafs around. Gawd knows 'ow 'e keeps out've the Army.' She paused again, and finished her coffee. 'That's wot Sam said. *And* 'e said 'e wished *you* wasn't in the Army.'

'I think I'm out of it for long enough,' said Rollison, thoughtfully.

'Are yer?' demanded Lizzie, and her eyes glowed. 'Are yer really? 'Strewth, that'll warm 'is 'eart, that will. Cor, bless me soul, 'ave I bin wantin' to hear that!'

There was a possibility that Lizzie had been followed, and since Rollison had been attacked so near to Scotland Yard her shadowers would assume that he was as hostile to them as the police; perhaps more so. He did not want an example made of her, she had suffered more than enough already. He decided to send Jolly with her to the 'Lion', and to follow them.

Apparently Jolly had anticipated the arrangement, for he came from the kitchen carrying his bowler hat and umbrella.

There was a taxi-rank not far from Gresham Terrace. Jolly made sure that two cabs were there before hiring the first. There was a pause

54

while Lizzie encouraged her bulk in, and from twenty yards away Rollison heard the springs groaning, followed by a jocular protest by the cabby.

Rollison took the second cab, with a brief 'Follow them'. From the rear window he watched for any sign of pursuit, but there was none. As far as he had been able to judge in the black-out, no one had watched the flat, and he began to feel that Lizzie had staged her sortie successfully. Her refusal to go to the police proved what he had believed for a long time past—that the suspicion between the police and the people of her world would never be completely dispersed. The blitz and the war in general had brought them closer together; there was more fraternizing and a greater trust. Yet Lizzie still sheered away from the police, for the penalty for squealing was a heavy one.

In the course of twelve hours, reflected Rollison, he had learned of three distinct aspects of the black market trading. Aunt Matilda as a buyer, Lett and Lizzie as sellers, and the police as the judiciaries. Other angles had also been presented, not the least being Livy's, at the Regal. Only then did he really begin to assess the immense range over which the market spread. He began to understand much more clearly why Grice was eager for help.

Inevitably he approached a question which he had not put to Grice, since Grice obviously could not answer it.

Why had Melsom been killed?

Melsom had been found in the river, but he might have been thrown in two or three miles from where his body had been discovered. He had last been seen near the Minories. Somewhere between that spot and the place where he had been killed the sergeant must have made a discovery of over-riding importance, for only a serious threat to their security would have induced the black marketeers to kill a policeman.

'All of which is obvious, and I'm empty of ideas,' mused the Toff.

Occasionally the pale orbs of cars approaching in the opposite direction glowed, but there was very little light. He had both windows down yet felt too warm, although there was a pleasant breeze on his cheeks. The cab went slowly and cautiously, the driver feeling his way round every corner. There was no sign of stars, and the clouds were glowering.

From a long way off there came a rumble which might have been gunfire but was more likely thunder. A flash of lightning, also far distant but showing the tall buildings of the City—he was in Fenchurch Street—confirmed the guess.

The cab passed Aldgate Pump to the accompaniment of another sheet of lightning, much more vivid. Soon after it a rumble of thunder cracked, nearly overhead, while a spattering of rain fell on the roof of the cab.

None of those things held Rollison's attention.

There was a glow of light ahead of him, reddish in the darkness and spreading much farther about the sky than he liked to see. It reminded him of the fires of London when he had been there at the tail-end of the blitz period. He sat forward in his seat and peered ahead.

The fire was in Aldgate High Street, on the left-hand side and before the junction of roads in front of Whitechapel Church; in short, near the 'Lion'.

As they drew nearer it was possible to see the flames, stark and vivid and voracious against the dark sky, and the figures of men in front of them, dark moving silhouettes. He was oblivious of the rain, now coming heavily, and of the rumbles in the sky; he stared towards the fire, and while he was doing so the cabby leaned back, opened the glass partition, and said:

'Looks like the old "Lion's" got it, sir, don't it?'

'Yes,' said Rollison bleakly. 'Yes. Get as near as you can and wait for me.'

CHAPTER SIX

BLACKIE IS AFRAID

A policeman in a steel helmet stopped the taxi. Drawn into the kerb was Jolly's cab, and Lizzie was squeezing herself out of it. Rollison jumped out before his cab stopped moving.

Heat from the flames struck him like a wall, making him gasp. He heard the hissing of water from emergency fire pumps already in operation, and from farther away there came the clamour of another fire-engine. The rain developed into a deluge, hissing on to flames which were roof high and shooting further and further towards the sky. Steam and smoke were rising and merging, men were shouting.

By one wall a fire-escape was being run up.

Rollison reached Lizzie as she finally extricated herself from her cab and cried:

'Gawd, Sammy's in ther! Gawd, where's Sammy? Save Sammy for me!'

'Lizzie—' began the Toff.

She swung round on him.

'Don't stand there! Save my Sam; get my Sam!' She began to run towards the burning pub, evading a fireman who tried to stop her. The flames showed through her hair like glowing tongues, a spray of water from the hose drenched her, but she lumbered on.

Rollison caught up with her, gripped her arm so that she could not free herself, and forced her to turn about.

Jolly and a policeman reached them.

'Sam! Sam!' shrieked Lizzie. 'Oh, 'e'll burn, 'e'll burn!'

She began to curse 'them', the people who had started the fire. She shook her fists and shouted and cried, while Rollison stepped to the captain of the fire-squad and made himself heard through the roar of the flames and the hissing of the rain.

'Have you got anyone out?'

'There.' A foghorn voice only just made itself heard. 'There's a sick man in that room; they're trying to get him now.'

The flames were licking about the top of the escape, on which two men were standing. One of them was smashing at a window with his axe. He disappeared, while Rollison stood by, knowing there was nothing he could do.

He caught sight of the man in black.

It happened suddenly, when he was not thinking of the man but only of Lizzie and her piteous cries and the possible fate of Sam Diver.

The man in black was standing not twenty yards away, watching the conflagration and heedless of the drenching rain. High above them a roll of thunder threatened to split the heavens, a fork of lightning made everything vivid.

59

Rollison watched the man, who was staring at the top of the ladder. So were a dozen or more other people, all just beyond the ring of firemen, who were laying out their hoses and would soon have the fire under control. Rollison watched the water spraying onto the adjoining buildings, while the blazing one was almost neglected.

The man in black turned.

Rollison doubted whether he was observed, for the man moved away, lowering his face then against the rain. Rollison slipped past him.

Jolly was standing with an arm about Lizzie's waist, an incongruous sight.

'Settle with my cabby,' Rollison said in passing.

The light was good enough to enable him to follow his quarry, whose going might be a deliberate ruse to get him away. He took that chance, and strode across the road. His man walked with long, raking strides, but remained a clear silhouette for some distance. Dozens of people were about, and others were streaming towards the scene of the outbreak.

The man in black turned into the Mile End Road.

Soon they were out of range of the fire-light, but the lightning was almost continuous; the noise of thunder and the pelting rain were enough to ensure that Rollison's progress was undetected. He kept within twenty yards of the man, always hugging the wall, gasping now and again when a gust of wind struck him. He was wet through, and rain was seeping down his neck; he could feel it clammy against his chest and back.

When the lightning revealed his quarry he saw also the rain which struck the road and bounced up again a foot or more. He was walking through water, his trousers were drenched, his feet squelched inside his shoes.

The other, walking steadily, passed half a dozen side turnings, then crossed the road and went down a narrow street to the right. Eventually this led to the river; but also it went past rows of cottages which had escaped the devastation of the blitz. Vague light showed 'S' signs and arrows, but there was no light except the flashes, the glare of which so affected Rollison's eyes that he could not see at all after them; the Stygian gloom had an eerie blanketing effect.

The chase was soon over, then, for Blackie turned into one of the little houses.

Rollison stopped ten yards behind the man. There was a pause while Blackie took a key from his pocket and fumbled for the lock.

By then Rollison was within two yards of him, and as the door opened he went forward swiftly and gripped the man's shoulder. His fingers slipped off wet clothes, but the man turned a little and staggered, taken completely by surprise. His face was only a pale blur, and

61

the Toff struck him. The blow landed on the side of the chin and sent the man lurching against the wall.

He was so unprepared that he made no effort to defend himself, but sagged helplessly, his arms by his sides. Rollison hit him again, this time an uppercut. He heard the man's teeth click together, and the other fell to the streaming pavement.

Breathing hard through his mouth, Rollison stepped into the narrow passage of the house, and raised his voice:

'Anyone at home?' He paused and shouted again: 'Anyone at home?'

There was no answer.

Rollison turned, bent over his victim and dragged him into the passage. He closed the street door before using his torch, so that he could see to open another door which led to the right.

The room beyond was shrouded in darkness.

Rollison dragged the man inside, and examined him in the light of his torch. His breathing was heavy, it was reasonable to think he would be unconscious for another five minutes; even if he came round he would be in no state to help himself.

Keeping the torch switched on, Rollison stepped back into the passage. There was an odour in the house, which he knew would have another room and a kitchen downstairs, three tiny bedrooms up. He had often been a 'guest' in similar homes, as often been disgusted by the condition of many of them. East End housewives could be, and often were, houseproud—but most of their hovels should have been condemned a decade before.

The back room and the scullery were empty. Rollison switched on a light, finding that the black-out was in position; it consisted of black paper blinds.

The room was not badly kept, but he wasted little time inspecting it before hurrying up the stairs. Every step he took water oozed over his shoes; he appeared to be wading all the time. Once or twice he gave an involuntary shudder.

The three upstairs rooms were also empty.

They too were clean enough, furnished with utility contemporary furniture—windows of shops in the Mile End Road were filled with exact replicas. It had the appearance of being a newly furnished home, for the wallpaper was also fresh and clean.

'Paperhanger's paste,' he said aloud.

He made sure that the doors were locked and bolted before returning to the front room. When he switched on the light he saw that Blackie was recovering.

For the first time the Toff was able to scrutinize him.

The earlier impression of a thin, rather haggard face was confirmed. The man's cheeks were hollow, his face bony and gaunt. There was a touch of the sinister about him even in his helplessness.

Rollison went down on one knee and ran through his pockets. They were empty. By the time the search was finished, the other's eyes were wide open; he made no attempt to move, but looked dazedly about him.

There was a cheap carpet, a settee and two easy chairs, a few oddments of furniture, and on the mantelpiece a walnut clock, too large, so that it looked likely to over-balance. Abruptly it chimed three, and the noise startled Rollison.

The man kicked out at his legs.

Rollison saw the kick coming, and skipped aside. Without speaking he bent down, gripped the lapels of his coat and hauled him to his feet, then pushed him into one of the easy chairs. Blackie flopped down, gasping. His eyes remained wide open; their dark glow gave the same sinister impression as the rest of his face, but there was something more: they were beginning to show fear and uncertainty.

For the first time he opened his lips. His voice was a croak.

'What—what are you doing?'

The Toff had taken off his hat. He held it in his hand, then threw it towards the man, who shrank back.

Standing there, pale in the bright light, his eyes cold and his chin set, there was much in the Toff to frighten. He maintained his deliberate silence, to play on the other's nerves. He believed this was a chance which he might never get again, for there was nothing to indicate that the other would be nervous unless he was in acute danger.

'*What are you doing?*' The voice rose a key.

Rollison stepped to the fireplace.

In front of it was a cheap plywood firescreen, and in the grate was red crepe paper. He pulled the paper out and put it in the middle of the floor, then broke the screen into several pieces across his knee. With them laid across the paper he pulled the settee and the other easy chair close to the heap, paused for a moment, and stared at the man in black. Blackie's lips were working.

Rollison took a petrol lighter from his pocket.

He was afraid that the damp might make the instrument difficult to light. Instead, it caught at the first flick of his finger. He held it steady and knelt by the paper, taking the light steadily towards it.

'*Stop! Stop that!*'

The other's shout was frenzied, his eyes were glaring. He moved from his chair, but with his free hand the Toff pushed him back. He groaned, and Rollison stood up without setting the paper on fire, and opened his lips for the first time.

'Doesn't death by fire appeal to you?'

'Don't—don't do it!' Blackie's voice was high-pitched, his face was working. 'You must be mad, mad!'

65

'I was quite sane when I saw the "Lion" burning, and heard Lizzie Diver screaming for her husband, who was helpless in a room nearly impossible to reach. You didn't give Diver much chance when you fired the "Lion".'

'You *must* be mad!'

'I'm under a strain, perhaps. I forgot to look after you first. You're not running away from this fire.' Rollison took out his revolver and slowly and deliberately turned it so that he held it by the barrel. He made a feint for the other's head. 'I mustn't hit too hard. If there's enough of you left they might realize it was no accident.'

'Rollison!' For the first time the man revealed that he knew his tormentor. He kept one hand up to fend off a blow from the gun, and held the other out supplicatingly. 'Rollison, you don't know what you're doing. You'll never get away with it.'

'The police won't think of me,' said Rollison harshly.

'I don't mean the police, I mean my friends!'

'They can't know you as well as I do. If they could see you cringing now they'd be glad I'd finished you off.'

He flicked the lighter again, and turned.

It was touch and go then; he knew that the other had recovered from the initial shock and probably from his earlier fears. So Rollison let the paper catch, then moved back as it

66

flared up.

'Put it out. Put it out! I'll tell you everything, I'll tell you what I know.'

'I don't think you know enough,' said the Toff evenly. 'I think there's just one way of dealing with you—and with Lett, Lowe, and the others. It's what the Nazis call "extermination", and it often happens to rats. I'll get you one at a time until I've smoked the last of you out.'

The wood was catching, the room was filling with smoke. He counted on the other's mounting horror to start a torrent of words.

'Stop it! *Stop it!*' Blackie made another effort to leave the chair, but Rollison pushed him back. There was a moment of tension while he stared into the leaping flames, and they reflected on his dark eyes. Then the flood burst.

'I can tell you who killed Melsom! It was Barbicue, Barbicue. He's after you; he told me to have you watched, to start the attack on you. He started the fire, I didn't. It's Barbicue, I tell you; he's the man you want—Barbicue! Melsom saw him and found out he was in it. That's why Melsom was killed. I said it was crazy, I wanted to stop him! Rollison, put the fire out, put it out!'

'Where does Barbicue live?' asked the Toff.

The carpet was singeing and black smuts were floating about the room. Flames were rising from the back of the chair, and would soon be beyond control.

'You'll find him at the Splendide Hotel. I can't tell you any more. Rollison, put it out!'

Rollison overturned the burning chair so that its back fell on the main fire and temporarily subdued it. He went into the kitchen, and filled a large enamel bowl with water. By the time he was back Blackie was on his feet, stamping out some of the flames.

Rollison pushed the chair aside, then emptied the bowl over the fire. Blackie was gasping with a mingling of relief and fear, but he acted promptly enough on Rollison's orders, took the enamel bowl, refilled it, and came hurrying back with water slopping over the sides. The room was pungent with the stench of burnt fabric, filled with the hiss of steam; but the fire had never reached great pretensions, and the task of quelling it was comparatively light.

Finished, Rollison said: 'What's your name?'

'L-Lett.' The man made no attempt to argue.

'Edward Lett?'

'No, no, I'm his brother! Rollison— Rollison, get me away from here! Barbicue will know I've squealed, he'll know I've told you! I'm not safe. Do you hear me?' The face which had looked sinister was now twisted in dread, and the Toff watched, feeling a deep contempt for the brother of Edward Lett, but a great interest in the man Barbicue, who could inspire such fear.

'Yes,' said the Toff slowly, 'I'll get you away; we've much to talk about yet.'

'Hurry!' gasped Lett. 'Hurry! They're bound to have followed you, they'll be here soon.'

CHAPTER SEVEN

BARBICUE

Rollison did not ask why the man had been so frightened if he expected Barbicue to follow so swiftly; or, more probably, friends of Barbicue.

He rolled the name over his tongue. It had a romantic ring; was no name for a rogue unless it were a gallant one, and in this business there was no gallantry.

Outside the rain was heavy, but the storm had passed except for distant rumbles and vague flashes in the sky. The Toff sent Lett ahead of him and followed close behind. They walked with their faces down to avoid the driving wind.

Lett made no effort to get away until they reached the end of the street; then he swung towards the left, jumping into the roadway.

The Toff stood still, and watched him go.

He was swallowed up in the darkness, but his padding footsteps echoed for some seconds. On the Toff's face there was a half-smile. He shivered and went on, pulling up abruptly when other footsteps sounded. He dropped his hand to his gun, but the voice which came was familiar and reassuring.

'I presume, sir,' said Jolly, 'that you intended to let him go?'

The words just carried to Rollison's ears. He could see his man-servant, a vague shape and a vaguer face. He shouted 'Yes,' and together they rounded the corner and walked more swiftly towards Aldgate, for the wind was no longer blowing directly into their faces.

After a few minutes, Rollison shouted:

'What about Sammy?'

'Safe, sir.'

Rollison nodded, an acknowledgement of which Jolly was quite unaware, and nothing more was said until they reached the scene of the fire.

'Lizzie and Diver have gone in here, sir,' said Jolly.

He stopped outside a shop a few doors removed from the 'Lion', which by the morrow would be just a black shell. The shop door was open, and a man stood in the middle of it when they entered, just visible against a faint glow of light.

Lizzie was still hysterical, and they were getting her to bed. No, she was not yet undressed. Undressing her would prove something of a problem, thought the Toff.

He was allowed a word or two with her, finding her much quieter than he had expected.

70

He left after making sure that Sam Diver had suffered no serious relapse; the doctor was still with him. Rollison took the name and address of the doctor and then hurried for a taxi. In less than half an hour he was in his bathroom, and Jolly in the kitchen, both stripping. Water was running for hot baths.

They said little until they had bathed. Jolly had prepared more coffee, and brought two cups into the lounge.

It was nearly five o'clock.

'Exactly twelve hours after I received the telephone message, sir,' said Jolly. 'The speed of events is frequently quite beyond my understanding; there are times when I agree with some of your friends, that you positively attract trouble.'

'You ought to know by now that it's the trouble that attracts me,' said Rollison, sipping his coffee.

'I found myself asking one particular question on our way back, sir.'

'What was it?'

'Why did you allow the man to leave you in the Mile End Road?'

'Because I staked our all that he had told me everything he could. He gave me a name that smacks of the Middle Ages, a name no one could invent on the spur of the moment. Barbicue. Does it mean anything to you?'

'I have a faint recollection that it refers to a roasted ox,' murmured Jolly.

71

'You're far too much of a materialist. Whatever else, it doesn't sound like a roasted ox. Why should Lett think of one, anyhow?'

'Lett, sir?'

'The name of the man in black. I'll call him Blackie, or he'll get confused with Mr Edward,' said Rollison, and went on to explain.

'I agree more than ever with the theory that you attract trouble, sir, but perhaps that is a fine point which hardly needs discussion now. This Barbicue should be at the Splendide Hotel, if Blackie is right.'

'The trouble is that I'm tired and you're tired,' said Rollison. 'If either of us visits Barbicue now we shall only make a hash of it. We could telephone to find out if there's a man with the name staying there.'

'I'll do it now, sir.' Jolly rose promptly. 'How much do you propose to tell the police?'

'Not everything, yet.'

'Not of Barbicue?'

'Certainly not Barbicue. The only evidence I have that there is such a man engaged on the black market, is the word of a rogue whom I third-degreed, and I don't know where to find him again. There's nothing to tell the police, yet.'

Jolly said, 'Excuse me, sir,' for he had finished dialling. He asked the necessary question of the night operator at the Splendide,

72

a mammoth hotel in the West End, paused, and then said, 'Thank you,' and replaced the receiver.

'There is a Mr Barbicue staying there,' he announced. 'He returned only about half an hour ago, and his room is Number 547.'

'I think we can safely leave him for a few hours,' decided Rollison.

'I could go and watch the hotel, sir.'

'No,' said Rollison firmly, 'you get some sleep. We don't want him alarmed just yet, anyhow.'

'I don't doubt, sir,' said Jolly, knowingly, 'that you have as good a reason for leaving Barbicue for the time being as you did for allowing Blackie Lett to go. What time would you like a call?'

'I'll have some tea at ten o'clock if I'm not about earlier.'

It was then a little past six.

Rollison was not surprised that he was awakened by Jolly, with tea and the morning papers, at ten o'clock precisely. Jolly did not look fresh-eyed; but then he rarely did. He was brisk enough as he poured tea and left two papers folded on the tray, then went out to run Rollison's bath. Rollison sipped the hot, weak tea, and cast one eye on the headline of an inside page of the *Cry* which Jolly had doubtless carefully selected for him. It was a heavy headline, reading:

73

BLACK MARKET MUST BE SMASHED GROWING MENACE REVEALED

There followed a short but accurate summary of the activities of the market, hinting vaguely that the police knew the names of the criminals but for some 'unexplained reason' could take no action. There followed a demand for immediate results.

'We'll try to oblige,' murmured the Toff, and climbed out of bed.

An hour later, bathed, shaved, dressed and breakfasted, and musing that Jolly had made a good job of pressing his uniform, he left the flat. Jolly had instructions to telephone inquiries about Lizzie and Sam, and Aunt Matilda.

The storm had eased the sultry heat of the heat-wave, but outside the sun was shining.

When he entered the foyer of the Splendide, a host of people were besieging the cashier's desk, or waiting for their bills. There was nothing restrained about the Splendide. It was London's biggest and most palatial hotel, and it screamed the facts in advertisements and in the red and gold of the foyer, lounges and dining-rooms. Calm and unflustered girls worked behind the reception desks to satisfy demands for speed and yet more speed in the presentation of bills, the lifts were working at pressure, a constant stream of people entered and left the main revolving doors. The

74

Splendide was not a hotel where the porters or the reception clerks would know off-hand the name of a client unless it were someone of exceptional importance. Only casually and without much hope did Rollison ask a uniformed and beribboned commissionaire whether he knew Mr Barbicue.

'Oh *yes*, sir,' said the commissionaire, who did not know the Toff. 'He's in the restaurant, having a late breakfast. You know he doesn't see anyone until after twelve o'clock, don't you?'

'I didn't,' admitted Rollison.

'That's his rule, sir.'

'That sounds as if he has visitors in shoals,' said Rollison.

'He has enough, sir, that's a fact.' The commissionaire was expansive between intervals of opening the doors leading to the lounge and closing them again.

Mr Barbicue had visitors by the score, it seemed, both men and women, in uniform and out of it. The commissionaire did not know for certain, but believed that Mr Barbicue had a business somewhere in the Midlands and was conducting it from the Splendide until he was able to find some London offices, which were practically unobtainable in the City or the West End.

Rollison thanked the man and strolled to the far end of the foyer. That he had been inquiring for Barbicue did not greatly matter; the commissionaire might report it, but as Barbicue's visitors were so numerous the inquiry would hardly strike him as unusual. Rollison waited until the commissionaire's attention was distracted by a request for information of two oldish ladies, before going to a lift.

There was no difficulty in finding his way to Room 547, for directions adorned the walls at every corner. Chambermaids and cleaners were busy in the passages, and most of the room doors were open. Rollison reached 547, wondering how he could best bluff his way into Barbicue's apartment.

The door was open. A maid was picking up some oddments from the floor and putting them in a wastepaper basket. She left the room with the basket, without closing the door, and hurried to her cupboard.

Rollison stepped into the room.

It was empty; so was the next one, reached through a communicating door standing wide open. There were two single beds in the first, but the second was furnished as a lounge-cum-study-or-office. There were several easy chairs, two tables, one of them piled with papers and holding a typewriter, and even a small filing-cabinet. On the cabinet were several weighty books, directories of parts of Greater London.

Rollison pushed the communicating door to and sat in one of the easy chairs, crossing his legs and lighting a cigarette.

The maid entered the other room, then pushed his door more widely open.

She stopped on the threshold.

'Mr Barbicue asked me to wait here,' Rollison said easily. 'As the door was open I came in.'

'That's all right, sir, but you did give me a start.' She deposited the wastepaper basket by a table, and hurried out. Rollison smiled at an ease of entry which was not really surprising in that mammoth abode in view of Barbicue's frequent visitors, and contemplated the windows opposite.

Barbicue's rooms were on the inside of the hotel, which was built in the shape of a triangle. The domed glass roof of the lounge was below, in sight when he stepped to the window and looked down. The dirty white stone of walls with countless windows, most of them wide open, were everywhere; it was no place for a man who wanted to get out of a window and escape in a hurry.

He returned to his chair, from which he could see the window opposite him. Someone was moving to and fro, but the net curtains at the window prevented him from deciding whether it was a man or woman. His ears were cocked for any sound of approach to 547, but he puzzled over the identity of the man or woman near the opposite window.

The net curtains were drawn back, and a girl stood by the open window for a moment, looking out and directly across to Barbicue's room. Rollison tried to persuade himself that it was imagination, but she appeared to take much more than a normal interest in the window.

It was rare for Rollison to be impressed by beauty; much of the disapproval of his family was due to his reputation as a philanderer, one not wholly justified but certainly not lacking cause. It was some time since his blood had been stirred by a woman as it was by this girl.

Strictly speaking, she was not beautiful, but she was extraordinarily good to look at, dark-haired and with a smooth complexion perhaps accentuated by the distance. She might have been a refined, a very refined, Lizzy Diver. She had Lizzie's colouring, a hint of Lizzie's vitality. She wore a vivid yellow blouse or jumper, with short sleeves, and he could see the waist of a dark skirt.

Abruptly she turned away.

Again Rollison persuaded himself that it was imagination that her lips had tightened as she did so, that she had made a gesture almost of anguish. When she had gone, Rollison rubbed his chin, stubbed out a cigarette and took another from his case.

He wished he could get the girl's face out of his mind, but it persisted in obtruding, and once when footsteps neared the door he ignored them until they were actually past, instead of being prepared for them to stop. He

78

shifted his chair into a position where he could see both the door leading from the passage and that between the two bedrooms, and tried to put thought of the girl from his mind.

Footsteps came dully, perhaps for the tenth time in as many minutes. There were men's voices, also. The footsteps stopped outside. Rollison sat up a little in his chair, but his face showed no change of expression although for the first time his mind was quite free from contemplation of the girl in the window.

A key chinked, then rattled against the keyhole of the bedroom. The door opened and the footsteps grew much closer, much louder. A smooth, mellow voice, surely that of a man who was used to the platform and could sway audiences with his tongue, for even in the ordinary sentence he used it sounded persuasive, said:

'Who is coming this morning, David?'

'There are only two appointments,' answered 'David', and then his words trailed off, for the other door had opened and the first speaker saw the Toff, and stood stock still.

CHAPTER EIGHT

OF THIS AND THAT

The Toff had the advantage of surprise, yet he was compelled to admit that Barbicue recovered with praiseworthy speed. Only for a moment did he lose countenance; then he advanced slowly, saying:

'Wait in there, David.'

No startled 'What the devil!' or 'Who are you, sir?' but a calm *Wait in there, David.* He half-turned the second man back to the bedroom so that Rollison caught only a glimpse of a high, shiny forehead.

Rollison spoke first, mildly and with some humour.

'I'm going to be disappointed if you're not Barbicue.'

There was a glimmer of a smile on the truly handsome countenance.

'You will not be disappointed on that score,' said Barbicue. He put his right hand into his pocket, drew out a slim gold cigarette case, advanced towards Rollison and proffered the case.

Rollison stubbed out his second cigarette and took a third.

'Which end is poisoned?' he asked.

'Both,' said Barbicue.

He was nearly as tall as the Toff, with powerful shoulders fitted perfectly by his coat; his tailor was an artist, perhaps even a genius. The suit was of medium grey, and in so big a man a positive creation, for it concealed any incipient *embompoint* while it supplied a touch of perfection, hinting at opulence and wealth, yet retaining good taste. His complexion was fair and very good, his hair was dark with streaks of iron grey. Wide-set eyes grew beneath a wide forehead, a broad nose—and breadth was needed on his round face—lips well-shaped and peculiarly red, and a chin made a little less prominent because of a somewhat fleshy jowl.

'Thanks,' said Rollison, and supplied a light. 'Good morning, Barbicue.'

'Good morning,' said Barbicue.

The silence lengthened, both men staring, as if willing the other to go on. It was a pause for mutual assessment. Rollison was quite sure that Barbicue would never forget him—and certainly he would never forget Barbicue.

'And now perhaps we can get to business,' said Barbicue at last. It was a minor triumph to have forced him into speaking. 'May I have your name, sir?'

'Rollison,' said Rollison.

'Major the Hon. Richard Rollison?'

'I'd no idea that I was so well known. I'd hoped that—'

'A moment, Major Rollison,' interrupted

81

Barbicue. 'I should dislike it if you were under any misapprehension at all. I heard of you quite fortuitously a day or two ago. I was interested, as I am always interested in active and unorthodox men. I'm puzzled, Major Rollison. I understood that visits of this nature were reserved for'—he paused and smiled benignly—'persons suspected of crime. Was I mistaken?'

Rollison chuckled.

'Certainly not. I'd like to be able to tell you that I called just for the sake of meeting, but in fact I suspect you, Mr Barbicue, of various crimes and many. I'm a little vague about some of them, but not at all vague about others. The fire at the "Lion", for instance, and the murder of Melsom. That was in the nature of a mistake. Or don't you make mistakes?' He paused.

'Go on,' murmured Barbicue. 'I like being amused.'

Rollison chuckled again.

'I don't think you read enough about me, or else you inquired too little. I can't recall any case of a man being amused when hearing his death sentence. Or have I missed something in Criminal Court records?'

'I know so little about crime,' said Barbicue urbanely. 'I thought you were the expert.'

'A dabbler, nothing more and nothing less—a *dilettante,* but sometimes prescient. I've worked with the police for a number of

82

years, and never known them fail to get their man. Trite but true, especially when C.I.D. officers are murdered. Not that you needed to have done that to get them busy; they were after you. It was just a matter of time.' Rollison paused, and flicked the ash of his cigarette. He was looking into Barbicue's eyes, seeing a coldness which matched his own. He went on slowly, as if searching for words. 'The difference is this, Barbicue. The English conception of treason is outmoded; until you killed Melsom the worst that could have happened to you was seven or ten years in prison. Now that Melsom is dead you will be hanged.'

Barbicue did not stir.

'Do I understand you to say that you think that, granted my complicity in the death of this man Melsom, you believe yourself capable of proving it against me?'

'Not necessarily. Someone will, and I hope to help.'

'I see,' said Barbicue.

'I wonder if you do,' said Rollison. 'On the whole I doubt it. If you were ten times as powerful, twenty times as rich, a hundred times as clever as you are, the police would get you. If I believed differently,' went on Rollison, putting a hand to his holster and unfastening it, 'I should kill you now. I liked Happy Melsom.'

The movement of the revolver to his hand was so swift that he doubted whether Barbicue knew what he was about to do. As the snout of the gun pointed towards the other, Barbicue backed away in alarm.

'Put that away, you idiot!'

'I'll keep it where it is, I prefer to feel safe.'

Barbicue said thinly:

'You are acting like a mountebank.'

'You mean buffoon. I'm just confirming the sentence, Barbicue, and telling you that if the police should be too long in catching you I'll hasten your end. Get it into your handsome head that you will soon be dead. By a noose or by a bullet really doesn't matter.'

'Presumably you *are* sane.' Barbicue had recovered, but there was a beading of perspiration on his forehead and his upper lip. With a deliberate movement he took a white silk handkerchief from his pocket and dabbed his forehead, then ran it along his lips and the side of his nose. 'It's too warm in here,' he said. 'I suppose you'll have no objection to my opening the window?'

'Open it by all means,' invited Rollison.

Barbicue stepped across, pushed the window up, and leaned with his back against it. There was no noticeable breeze although by the window itself it was probably cooler. Rollison hitched his chair round, after seeing that there was a bolt on the door of the room. He could see past Barbicue to the window opposite, and also the communicating door, thus making sure that he could not be taken by surprise.

'Is that better?'

'I would like to know why you came,' said Barbicue.

'I came to tell you that I know you killed Melsom, or ordered his death. I know that you employ the Letts, that a great proportion of food and consumer goods which reach the public illegally passes through your hands, or at least is under your control. Shall I send you a note confirming all this?'

'There is no truth at all in your absurd accusations.' Barbicue eyed the gun, which was lying negligently against the Toff's right leg. 'Put that weapon away, and talk like an intelligent man. If you have been misinformed I want to know where you obtained your information. My business is perfectly legal.'

'I don't like wasting time,' said Rollison.

Barbicue looked towards the filing-cabinet.

'If you look in there you will find all the evidence you need.'

'I've given you some credit,' Rollison said.

He moved from his chair with a swift movement pantherish in its speed, and reached Barbicue as the man opened his lips. Whatever Barbicue was trying to say was cut short. Rollison gripped his right hand, and with a quick turn of the wrist made Barbicue stumble away from the window.

As Barbicue stumbled, Rollison sat heavily on the floor.

Neither of them heard the whang of the

bullet which came through the open window, but it banged into the wall above the filing-cabinet. Several small pieces of plaster flew about the room, and a sifting of powder covered the top of the cabinet.

A second bullet cracked against the wall an inch from the first.

Barbicue stumbled against a chair and recovered himself. Rollison regained his feet and for a moment stood outlined against the window, but there was no further shooting. He caught a glimpse of a movement in the room opposite, where the girl had been.

Before he had time to speak, while Barbicue was breathing heavily and staring at him and then at the wall, there was a loud knock on the communicating door, which opened abruptly. 'David' stood on the threshold. Rollison turned in time to see his lips gaping so that they showed a dark, almost black circle, as if he had no teeth.

Then Rollison stooped and picked up one of the bullets, which had fallen to the floor after striking a book; a glance told him it was a .22.

The other man was staring at the revolver. Barbicue roared at him:

'Get out; do as you're told!'

'After me,' said Rollison, and David staggered back as Rollison moved towards and past him, and then stormed out of Room 547 and into the passage. He turned right and

86

hurried, believing he had just a chance of catching the girl.

CHAPTER NINE

LADY IN YELLOW

Rollison saw her walking quickly towards the lifts.

By then he had replaced his revolver and fastened the flap, so that his progress no longer made the maids stop and stare. He slowed down as he recognized the dark hair and yellow 'blouse', which proved to be a shirt blouse over a pair of dark brown slacks. If the girl knew that he was following her she showed no alarm as she pressed the button marked 'DOWN' and stood back.

'Good morning,' said Rollison, not too brightly.

'Good morning.' She looked at him without a smile.

She had a steady enough nerve. At close quarters the bloom of her complexion was a rare and lovely thing, and her rather long, chiselled face might miss beauty but was striking. He saw her enormous dark lashes, and the casual way her black hair was drawn back from her forehead. It was glossy hair, wavy but not curly, with few loose strands.

'It keeps warm,' persisted Rollison.

'Doesn't it?' she said coldly.

'I wonder if the lift will be long?' said Rollison.

She drew a deep breath as the lift arrived, and a neatly-dressed lift girl said:

'Going down.'

Rollison waited for the girl to enter.

He glanced over his shoulder, for there were footsteps along the passage, and the lift girl hesitated as she half-closed the doors. She even began to open them again, and through the opening Rollison saw Barbicue.

So did the girl in yellow.

A single glance at her face told Rollison that she had no desire to meet Barbicue; if a woman could show naked fear in a single glance, she did in that moment.

Rollison put a hand over the lift girl's as Barbicue drew nearer, and said convincingly:

'A pound note if you'll take us down alone.'

He helped to push the door, which closed as Barbicue drew within ten yards. The lift girl jerked the car once or twice before it reached the ground floor. Rollison took a pound note from his pocket and pressed it into her hand.

When the doors opened on the ground floor a little crowd was waiting. The girl stared at him before stepping out, and the lift attendant gasped her thanks.

Rollison put a hand on the girl's arm and hustled her through the foyer and into the street, which was close to Piccadilly. A commissionaire droned 'Taxi, sir?'

'Yes, in a hurry.'

The cab arrived, and there was no sign of Barbicue. Rollison helped the girl into the cab, told the driver to go to Gresham Terrace, and sat in a corner. The girl continued to stare at him without speaking. He believed that until then her chief emotion had been the fear which he had seen in her eyes at the sight of Barbicue; but now she was beginning to think about him.

'Well, that's not too bad,' he opined. 'A really good morning, after all. You shoot quite well, don't you?'

'What are you talking about?' She had to school her voice to make the question seem natural.

'You, and bullets, and Barbicue,' said Rollison.

'I—I've never fired a gun in my life.'

'Well, I don't see why we should argue,' conceded Rollison. 'It's no way to become friends. I haven't a lot of time to spare, and I think we ought to reach some kind of an understanding. I think you shot at Barbicue, and that it was attempted murder. Barbicue doubtless thinks so too, and I fancy he will go to the police about it. I've no love for Barbicue, and I'm well-disposed to those who dislike him.'

'I've never fired a gun in my life,' she insisted hotly.

'I'm putting it to you that Barbicue might

think differently,' persisted Rollison. 'I'm guessing that you don't like him, and presumably know something about him. I'd like you to tell me what you know. You wanted to get away from him, and I've helped you. In return I'd like your name and address. I'll come and see you later in the day, or you can come to see me.'

'I don't know that—' she began.

'No, don't argue,' said Rollison sharply. 'I haven't time for it.' He stretched out a hand and took a brown cloth-covered bag from beneath her arm. She tried to get it back, but he opened the bag. She snatched at it, and spoke angrily.

'Don't do that! You've no right!'

There was a notecase inside, and several other oddments, mostly of make-up accessories, and a purse. He put the notecase in his pocket, while she glared at him, not soothed at all by his conciliatory smile. She took the bag, and held out her other hand for the notecase.

'Give me that back. It's bare-faced robbery!'

Rollison leaned back and regarded her without a smile.

'If you want to see me before I come to see you, here's my address.'

He took a card from his wallet; it was an old one, giving his name and address on one side, and on the other decorated with some pencilled drawings of a top hat, a monocle and a swagger cane. It might be amateurish and even gawkish, but on occasions the timely use of the cards had brought welcome results.

The girl looked only on the printed side, appeared to resign herself to losing her notecase, and said in a brusque voice:

'Where are you taking me?'

'Wherever you wish to go,' Rollison assured her. 'I haven't yet been able to tear myself in two, and I must see Barbicue.'

'And of course you're going to tell him that you caught up with me.'

'He won't need telling. But I *had* thought of assuring him that you ran away from me! If you'd prefer me to think up a different story, just say the word.' Rollison paused. 'No? Too bad, but I suppose I mustn't expect everything at once. Where shall I tell the driver to take you?'

He knew that she did not believe he was going to let her choose her own destination, so tapped on the glass partition and told the driver to draw into the kerb. He got out as soon as the cab stopped, pausing for a moment in the doorway.

'I'll see you this afternoon, if Barbicue leaves enough of me to see anything. Don't prepare a faked story, will you? You'll feel much better after you've told the truth. Oh, and another thing. If you're suspicious of flats and don't want to risk visiting mine, go to Seven, Braddon Place and ask Lady Gloria Hurst to

91

let me know you're there.'

He closed the door, gave a ten shilling note to the driver, and said:

'Go wherever your passenger says.'

'Right you are, sir!'

Rollison turned back towards the Splendide, a few hundred yards away; some traffic blocks and one-way streets had made the short journey take a long time.

It occurred to him worryingly that he might have been followed, and the girl could have been shadowed, too. But he had had to take some risks, and he was very anxious to see Barbicue again.

Near the reception desk and the hall porter was the talkative commissionaire, who nodded affably.

'Has Mr Barbicue finished breakfast yet?' inquired the Toff.

'Oh yes, sir! He'll be able to see you now. George, ask him, will you?'

The hall porter telephoned Room 547, asking whether Mr Barbicue would see Major Rollison. A voice that was not Barbicue's reached the Toff's ears before the porter said:

'Will you go up, please?'

Rollison went leisurely to the lift, caught sight of an officer from a unit to which he had belonged before joining Travers, and was reminded that he should go to see his C.O. that day.

David opened the door.

Hitherto Rollison had gained only an impression of a large round face and a high forehead. Now he saw that David was a thin, weedy young man, immaculately dressed. The earlier impression was not far out, for David had a moon of a face and, if size was any criterion, his head had a capacity for vast mental profundities.

Just then David gulped, drawing attention to an Adam's apple lurking beneath his large collar, and asked Rollison to go in.

Barbicue was in the second room.

He was sitting in front of one of the tables, but pushed his chair back when Rollison entered. What was much more unexpected was his outstretched hand. Rollison was so surprised that he extended his.

Barbicue had a powerful grip.

'I'm really glad you returned, Major Rollison,' he said warmly. 'I was afraid you might prefer to leave the matter as it stood.'

'And you would hate me to labour under any illusions,' Rollison completed for him. 'You see, I read minds, I'm the modern Old Moore.' He sat down as Barbicue proffered cigarettes. 'Not now, thanks.'

'They're quite harmless, I assure you,' said Barbicue. 'But—no, I'm being flippant. Major Rollison, between you and me I am not really myself. That shooting incident caused me grave concern. I am not unaware of the debt I owe you.'

'No debt,' murmured Rollison. 'I'd rather make my own kill.'

'I won't argue with you. I won't even ask you where you got your fantastic ideas. I will just tell you that you are hopelessly wide of the mark. My work, as I have said before, is strictly legitimate. I have been giving considerable thought to the present strange situation, for I am prepared to go to any lengths to satisfy a man who has done me so great a service. If you are really convinced that there is any measure of truth in your accusations, I invite you to nominate any man—*any* man, yourself if you have the opportunity—to work with me. Say, for one month. Longer if you prefer it. I am not going to try to prejudice or persuade you.'

'That's a new idea,' Rollison admitted, frowning. 'I'll think about it.'

'Do,' said Barbicue earnestly. 'I shall be here for another three days, and then I shall return to the Midlands where I shall stay for perhaps two weeks before going to Scotland for five or six days. I will pay your nominee's salary and expenses, and he can be with me at all my interviews.' Barbicue was eyeing Rollison intently. 'He can live like a lord, Rollison!'

'Yes,' murmured Rollison. 'That's where we're constitutionally at variance; I don't see why anyone should live like a lord these days.'

'Now come, don't talk like a prig. Let me know within the next forty-eight hours, and I will arrange accommodation for your representative.' Rollison waited for him to add: 'I cannot say fairer than that,' but Barbicue went on in a more measured voice, giving a good imitation of an orator addressing a packed meeting.

'Now, Rollison, you actually saw this shooting?'

'Yes.'

'You may be surprised to know that I have not informed the police, and I am arranging for a workman to come and repair the wall. I am not by nature vindictive, and I desire no police solicitude over a matter essentially private.'

'Too bad,' interpolated Rollison; 'I thought of nominating a policeman.'

'I wish you wouldn't jest,' said Barbicue. 'I am perfectly serious about all this. I would prefer to keep the fact that I was attacked, quite secret, I know that it was attempted murder, of course, but there are circumstances in which even that should not be disclosed. The young woman whom you saw in the lift fired the shot, of course.' He paused.

'I didn't see her,' declared the Toff. 'I saw a hand holding a gun.'

'But she was directly opposite you.'

'The gun and the hand were,' said Rollison firmly. 'The rest were hidden behind the net curtains. She had been in the room a few minutes before, but there could have been someone with her, or someone could have entered the room after she left it.'

'Rollison, you don't really believe that.'

'It's a possibility,' argued Rollison.

'I am beginning to wonder whether your reputation is justified,' said Barbicue, as if speaking to himself. He waved a hand; it was long, slender, white, and manicured. 'I know she shot at me; she bears me great malice.'

'Why such malice?' inquired Rollison.

'She believes—' began Barbicue, and then stopped. 'No, Rollison, I won't insult you with fairy stories! I would like to help her, in point of fact. She needs a psychiatrist, urgently. Did she tell you where she is staying?'

'No.'

'What happened when you left here?'

'We took a taxi, and she jumped out at some traffic lights,' Rollison told him with a fine air of veracity. 'I hadn't really got my breath back.'

Barbicue appeared to believe him.

'I'm sorry about that. She is a charming young woman, and I think the proper psychiatric treatment would lead to full recovery.' Barbicue contemplated the Toff for some seconds and then shrugged his big shoulders. 'It cannot be helped, I've no doubt you did your best.'

Rollison stared. '*What's* that?'

Barbicue brushed the question aside; he might have been talking to David or to any other employee or dependent.

'In any case, I shall not have it on my

96

conscience that she was delivered into the hands of the police and forced to suffer a trial.' He tightened his lips. 'If you are tempted to report the shooting, I shall be forced to deny it.'

'You would make Ananias blush for shame,' said Rollison. 'Are you offering a reason for her malice, or do I have to guess?'

'I'm afraid it will sound fantastic,' said Barbicue. 'The child believes that I ruined her father. He and I were business associates, and he was foolish enough to trifle with the law on several occasions. I withdrew my share of the capital, and he was unable to maintain his business without it. Consequently he went bankrupt. He committed suicide. The Gerrard case—you may remember it.'

Rollison shook his head.

'I'm surprised at that,' Barbicue assured him, 'it happened about six months after the war started.'

'I was abroad,' Rollison explained.

'Gerrard's crash ruined a number of people, I am afraid; his affairs were in a deplorable state. I did what I could to salvage something for his daughter, but...' Barbicue laughed. 'It is difficult to understand the human mind, especially under a severe strain or after a shock, and her father's suicide was undoubtedly a shock.'

Barbicue's voice grew harsh. There was a different expression in his eyes, a wary one, making the Toff think that he was approaching the crux of his story.

'She told the police that it was my fault. They had to disillusion her, or endeavour to. My own affairs were in perfect order, of course; perfect order. But Angela would not have it, she made a point of seeing me and talking nonsense about retribution.'

Rollison started, and Barbicue stopped abruptly.

'What is the matter?'

'A realization,' said Rollison as if aghast, 'that Angela Gerrard and I have something in common.'

'Do you mean you remember her?'

'Not *l'affaire Gerrard*,' admitted Rollison, 'but we have the same thing in mind for you. Retribution, Barbicue; a good old English word. Not to say biblical. I must certainly try to find her.'

'If you persist in play-acting I shall get really annoyed,' said Barbicue. 'I am telling you exactly what happened because I feel that your providential intervention has saved my life. I am very fond of my life.'

'That's too bad,' said Rollison.

'Rollison, if—'

'—I persist you will get really annoyed. You said it before,' the Toff reminded him. 'I ignored it. I don't give a damn whether you're annoyed or not. I already wanted you for Melsom and the Divers as well as your filthy black marketeering. Now I want you for

Angela Gerrard's father.'

His voice was scathing, although his lips hardly moved. He looked straight into Barbicue's eyes, then turned towards the door.

CHAPTER TEN

THE MUNIFICENCE OF BARBICUE

'Rollison, come back immediately!'

Barbicue called out as Rollison reached the door. He rose from his chair and made as if to stride across the room. Rollison opened the door and stepped through, to find David standing in his path. He pushed David aside unceremoniously as Barbicue repeated:

'Rollison, come back!'

Rollison approached the second door. A scrambling sound followed, and he heard David panting by his side.

'He—he *wants* you.'

'He'll learn better,' said the Toff, and went out, slamming the door behind him.

The bleakness on his face disappeared as he strode along the passage, and he surprised a maid with a beaming smile. She stood staring after him, while he waited to hear Barbicue's footsteps. He reached the lift without pursuit.

The girl he had tipped so generously opened the doors as soon as the lift arrived.

'No special commissions this time,' said Rollison. 'But wait a moment, here's one. Had you seen that young lady before? The one who was in the lift with me, I mean.'

'I—I don't remember her very well, sir.'

'She was wearing a yellow blouse and brown slacks.'

'I—I wish I could remember, sir; I'd like to help you, but I haven't been on the lift long and I don't get used to faces very quickly. I *do* wish I could help you.'

Rollison went thoughtfully into the street, walking towards Piccadilly and seeing throngs of men and women who looked too hot to hurry, and yet by force of habit tried to. The sun was almost directly above Eros, who was sheltering coyly behind his wooden hoarding and National Savings posters. Heat radiated from the roadway, made itself felt even in the hoarse voice of the newsvendors.

He walked to his flat.

Jolly admitted him and excused himself hurriedly; something was in the oven. Rollison smiled and felt contented when he took off his tunic, then decided to change into grey slacks and a linen coat. After a wash and the change, Jolly had a diminutive roast joint on the table, and there was some lager.

'And how much did that bottle cost?' Rollison asked with a touch of grimness.

'The normal price, sir,' said Jolly. 'I hope you will find it cold enough.'

Rollison sampled it, and agreed that it was exactly the right temperature. Jolly retired after a satisfactory report on the Divers and Aunt Matilda, and Rollison ate and allowed his mind to rove over the events of the morning. He disliked the coincidence of his visit to Barbicue and the attempted shooting. For the rest, he was satisfied that his visit to Barbicue had been effective. In his more expansive moments he would lay claim to having originated the term 'psychological terrorism' and also the application of it. It was no more and no less than a commonsense application of fear, by degrees. He had told Barbicue enough to make the man think, and thinking was the first step to worry, worry was a close neighbour of over-eagerness to erase the source of the anxiety, particularly in men of the Barbicue *genre*.

He waited until Jolly had finished his lunch, then went into the kitchen, and while the servant was washing-up talked freely and graphically. Jolly inclined his head, and murmured an occasional 'Yes' and 'No'. When at last Rollison finished Jolly turned his large tired eyes towards him, and said:

'I should think you have every cause for satisfaction, sir.'

'I wonder if you're right.'

'I hardly see any cause for uncertainty,' Jolly assured him, polishing a glass assiduously. 'You may not have discovered any piece of

101

factual evidence against Barbicue, but you have gone to the fountain-head, if I may use the expression. I have little doubt that he will be very worried. I would call it a quite outstanding example of your methods. You desired to make Barbicue anxious and become uncertain of himself, to make him speculate upon how much information you have obtained about him. You have undoubtedly succeeded.'

'Yes,' conceded Rollison, lighting a cigarette.

'Are you smoking rather more than usual, sir?' asked Jolly ingenuously.

'If you mean "Aren't I smoking too much"?—no,' retorted Rollison. 'Unless there's an acute shortage of cigarettes,' he added hastily. 'I'd taken it for granted that—'

'I have a small store,' admitted Jolly. 'But in the past you have asked me to remind you if you appeared to be chain-smoking. Shall I ignore that order in future?'

Rollison put his head on one side.

'I don't believe I ever gave it, but I'm quite sure I couldn't stop you "reminding" me. What was I going to say?'

'I imagine you were going to reflect that you neglected an opportunity of finding out Barbicue's genuine business, which is unimportant since you can easily get the information.'

In fact Rollison telephoned a friend, more

accurately a friend of his father's, a criminal lawyer who would know all there was to know about the Gerrard case, and probably something about Barbicue. After some delay he was speaking to the senior partner in Lane, Shapley and Lane, although two clerks had assured him that Mr Andrew Lane was engaged with an important client and could not be disturbed.

'Hallo, Rolly,' said Lane, whose voice was bluff and downright as the man himself. 'Now that you've worked all my staff into a panic, it had better be good.'

Rollison chuckled.

'It's very good. It goes back to six months or so after the outbreak of war. A man named Gerrard, figuring in some *cause celebre*. You may not remember him, but—'

'Do you mean to say you hadn't heard of it?' asked Lane incredulously. 'A shocking business. I always liked Gerrard, but he had his affairs in a hopeless muddle, and I didn't blame him for taking the easy way out. You mustn't expect me to go into detail now, but I'm free for dinner this evening.'

'We'll call that arranged,' said Rollison. 'At the "Regal" if it's all right with you?'

'That'll do nicely. I'll see you about seven-thirty. Goodbye, and—'

'Not yet,' said Rollison hastily. 'There's another man. Barbicue, Christian name and forebears unknown, but a partner of Gerrard's

103

at one time.'

'He left Gerrard some time before the smash.'

'Any unsavoury information about him?'

'No-o,' said Lane uncertainly. 'A little distrust in some circles, but I don't think it provenly justified. Not that he's a man I like particularly.'

'D'you know him, then?'

'Yes, fairly well. I can introduce you, if that's what you're after,' said Lane.

'We've met,' Rollison said drily. 'What does he do?'

'What doesn't he do would be more on the mark,' said Lane. 'He was one of the few men who bought up some of London before the Government stopped bear selling after the bomb damage; that's where he first came into prominence. Since then he's specialized in buying land and property, particularly in London suburbs, and the Midlands. Is that enough for you to go on with?'

'Give me another hundred words on him,' pleaded Rollison.

'Do you need a hundred? He buys for cash, and occasionally lends cash on mortgage. He kept a London office until six months ago, when it was destroyed by fire. Since then he's operated from Birmingham, although he does business in London and other towns, often using a suite of rooms at one of the big popular hotels. He won't touch leaseholds, insists on

104

freeholds all the time, and pays well in cash. I can't tell you more than that just now,' went on Lane.

'For the time being that's plenty,' Rollison said gratefully. 'I'm going to the "Regal" to order that dinner.'

He rang off, turned from the telephone, and eyed Jolly, who was putting some cutlery into a drawer.

'Jolly,' he said. 'Barbicue is undoubtedly clever. In all my life I've never known of a better cover. He buys property, any kind of property, cash on signing the agreement or against deeds. His business is an open book; no wonder he asked for a nominee!' He slid both hands into his pockets and whistled a little above his breath the tune of 'Ah, Sweet Mystery of Life'. 'It explains why he travels here and there, it allows him to contact a host of people.'

'You won't forget to telephone Colonel Travers, sir, will you?' asked Jolly.

'Eh? Oh, no. I'll do it now.'

'Colonel Travers speaking,' said the leathery whippet a few minutes later.

'Rollison here, sir,' began Rollison, and lied, and then had to listen to commiseration and the hope that his aunt would soon improve. He hoped that if he was away for two or three days it would be all right.

'Yes, yes,' said Travers. 'I'm sorry to hear that she's no better. Good-bye, Rollison. Have a good time.'

Travers rang down.

Rollison cocked an eyebrow towards Jolly, and shook his head sadly.

'There's far too much cynical distrust in the world. "Have a good time" indeed!' He chuckled and felt warmly towards Travers before thinking again of Barbicue and what he had learned so quickly and so simply from Lane.

The front-door bell rang.

Jolly opened it, had a few words with the caller, and was asked to 'sign the third line'. He did, and then staggered into the lounge with a parcel which he rested gratefully on an easy chair. The parcel was well wrapped in stout brown paper and corded securely.

'We're getting almost pre-war,' said Rollison. 'What's that?'

'I've no idea, sir; it's addressed to you.'

'Tyepwritten label, two addresses, no name of sender. Ought we to be suspicious, Jolly? Booby-traps and infernal machines are no less effective for being received trustfully.'

'Had I been here on my own, sir,' said Jolly, 'I would have opened it without raising that query.' He was faintly disapproving, although there was precedent enough for the Toff's question. 'I'll take it into the kitchen—'

'We'll take it,' corrected Rollison.

The surface of the container beneath the paper was hard; when the cords were cut it was revealed to be wood; the contents were still hidden, the packing even more secure. They eyed it, and then Jolly took a claw-headed hammer from a small tool-box kept in the bottom of the airing cupboard.

'The explosion will probably occur at the lifting of the third nail,' said Rollison sombrely. 'Your will and all necessary formalities prepared, Jolly? If not the third, the fourth,' he amended as Jolly prised up nails expertly one by one.

A piece of board was free then at one end, and Rollison began to lift it.

'I think it would be wiser to use this hammer, sir,' said Jolly. 'Nails are scarce, and we had best not bend them.'

'I beg your pardon,' said the Toff humbly.

He watched with an interest not concealed by his facetious commentary, until the lid was off—actually three pieces of flat board—and a layer of closely packed wood-straw was revealed.

'Perhaps we're not going to die,' conceded Rollison. 'I'll give you three guesses, Jolly.'

'I am completely at a loss, sir,' Jolly declared, lifting the wood-straw out carefully and placing it on the brown paper to prevent litter. 'I—'

The top of a bottle was revealed.

'Well, well,' said the Toff. 'So we're to be poisoned.'

Gently, almost lovingly, Jolly removed a

bottle which was covered with dust and retained more than a suspicion of cobwebs. Reverently they regarded the label, which said modestly that the brandy was known as Louis de Salignac. Two other bottles followed, also of the cognac; three bottles of Bristol Cream joined the others on the small kitchen table.

'These are all virtually unobtainable, sir,' said Jolly, in a hollow tone.

'Virtually?' asked the Toff. 'Is anything else there?'

'I think so, sir.' Jolly delved again, to straighten up with two glass pots of caviare. Rollison retrieved some *pate de foie gras*. Jolly drew a boxed Stilton, Rollison a waxed container with at least two pounds of butter. The pile of shavings grew higher and the kitchen table was covered from corner to corner.

They dived and delved.

They pulled away the last of the straw, then found that the bottom of the case was filled with tins of cigarettes, a variety of brands, Turkish, Virginian and Egyptian in a proportion of three Virginian to one each of the others.

When the box was finally quite empty, the straw reached their knees, and the cigarettes were piled on the drainingboard.

'Well, well,' said Rollison again after a long silence, 'He forgot to send the roses and his love.'

108

'An astonishing selection, sir,' opined Jolly.

'Stupefying. Paralysing. Pulverizing. Incredible, Jolly, and all from Mr Barbicue.'

'I suppose that *is* their source?'

'Of course it's Barbicue.' Rollison was smiling as he looked into Jolly's eyes. 'It's typically Barbicue; it reeks of the man. He can't believe that I mean what I say. His mind is the type which works in deep-grooved channels, *a la* Goering. There is no subtlety in him, only a twisted cunning.' He raised a hand, finger pointing towards the ceiling. 'See, Major Rollison! This is but a token of what I can send you. You will not, you cannot, seriously intend to endeavour to cut off the source of such munificence. Have done with such nonsense, my friend, away with the buffoonery.'

'Very impressive, sir,' murmured Jolly. 'What shall I do with them?'

'Examine with due care,' said Rollison, 'and tuck 'em away somewhere for the time being; we'll find a soup kitchen or a Prisoner of War Society which will put them to good purpose.'

'Including the cigarettes?'

'We might try one box of the Virginians. There's a presence about that man, a magnificence. I wish he wasn't a born rogue. I wish—there's the doorbell again. Off you go.'

He contemplated the piles of rare delicacies while Jolly went to the door and again engaged in brief conversation. In a moment of alarm he thought that there was another parcel, and was halfway to the door when Jolly closed it, turning with a letter in his hand.

'A special delivery, sir, from Grey's Express Service.'

'I suppose we should have expected that,' said Rollison.

He opened the letter. It was typewritten and signed by Barbicue. The signature was imposing, the downstrokes heavy, each letter formed clearly with a characteristic quite its own.

My dear Major Rollison,

I was disturbed that we parted on terms which, on the surface, appeared to be antagonistic, yet I feel sure that on second thoughts we shall both come to realize that we were carried away by the heat of the moment.

I am looking forward with very great pleasure to receiving your representative to accompany me on my tour for the next month. I suppose it is too much to hope that you can spare a few days yourself?

Believe me, my dear Major, I found our two interviews stimulating and intriguing, and in spite of the unfortunate incident which so nearly made a further meeting impossible—I need not tell you what I mean!—I am sure that you feel the same.

I am, my dear Major,
Gratefully and sincerely yours,
Justin Barbicue.

110

Rollison handed the letter to Jolly without speaking. Jolly read it impassively.

'I gather, sir, that Mr Barbicue writes very much as he speaks.'

'Consistent if nothing else. Jolly this is an experience which stimulates *and* intrigues. No mention of the goodies; he's much too careful for that. I wish he had something to sell in the way of land or property, we might contact him better that way. But—'

'I hope you're not overlooking the obvious possibility,' Jolly said quietly.

Rollison shook his head.

'No, I don't think so. Barbicue would like to lull me into a sense of security. Would he do anything violent or hostile while he is wooing me like this? Of course not. He hopes I'll close my eyes to danger, and—Jolly!'

'Yes, sir.'

'We're talking in the purple. We must stop it.'

'I'll clear the kitchen table,' said Jolly, and left Rollison to sprawl in an easy chair, eyes narrowed, brow furrowed. He was beginning to feel the loss of sleep the previous night, and decided to turn in for an hour.

He stripped to singlet and trunks and lay on the bed, dozing fitfully. He was in the middle of strangling Barbicue with his right hand and punching Blackie Lett's nose with his left when Jolly shook his shoulder, and he woke to see

111

tea by the side of the bed.

He struggled up.

'Two mornings in one day!' He took a cup of tea. 'Give me a cigarette, will you?' Jolly obliged, and Rollison frowned towards the dressing-table, where he could just see his reflection. 'I've heard that forty winks in the afternoon precede middle age, but only just.'

'I hardly think that is a matter for concern, sir,' said Jolly gravely. 'Mr Churchill goes to bed in the afternoon. I would not have disturbed you, as it is not yet five o'clock, except that there is a message from Lady Gloria. She would like you to telephone her.'

'Oh, would she,' said Rollison.

He dialled at once, asked for Lady Gloria, and was soon listening to her with rapt attention.

'Richard,' said Lady Gloria ominously, 'I feel no resentment because you make this house a trysting-place, no particular objection to allowing wild-eyed young women to storm here and demand to see you. But I *object*,' added Lady Gloria much more ominously, 'I object very much indeed when the young woman's other suitor follows her and proceeds to disrupt the household peace. Do you mind coming here at once?'

'Not a bit,' Rollison assured her. 'I'll come as soon as I'm dressed. Hold 'em, Glory. Even if they fight like cats, hold 'em. They matter.'

'As soon as you're *dressed*?' Lady Gloria

112

drew a deep breath. 'Jolly told me you were out.'

'I gave him clear instructions,' said Rollison glibly. 'Anyhow I *was* out. I visited a far, far better world, where I was strangling people all over the place. The only thing I didn't do was to eat tinned salmon. If you know where that salmon has jumped you'd be surprised.'

CHAPTER ELEVEN

ANGELA

Angela had a quarrelsome suitor; of course, Rollison should have thought of a suitor long ago. He had given only passing attention to too many things.

From the starting point of Angela's deep malice there was a chain of events divorced from the black martketting but at one time almost certainly married to it. The Barbicue-Gerrard quarrel, followed by Gerrard's suicide and Angela's conviction that Barbicue was to blame might have led to the shooting attempt in the Splendide.

Another factor also slipped into perspective—a remark of Grice's when he had told his story.

'I'm inclined to wonder whether there aren't two organizations working against each other.'

113

If Grice knew of the shooting he would think that further evidence of two groups. There was yet another matter: had the fire which had gutted Barbicue's office in London and driven him to using hotel suites been accidental or malicious?

'Malicious and with forethought,' said the Toff *sotto voce*. 'Matilda, Matilda, you know not what you've done.'

There was a scar at the corner of Braddon Place, where two houses had been demolished by bombs, and Rollison had not yet grown used to the sight. Momentarily it took his mind off the main subject, but as he paid his taxi driver and walked up the four stone steps to the front door of Number 7 he was reminded by a carrying voice from the open window.

'I don't believe Rollison's on the way,' a man declared. 'You've tricked and cheated me. I'll never forgive you for it, never.'

Patton was opening the door as he knocked. He was tight-lipped and silent as Rollison entered and said good afternoon. As tight-lipped and unbending he took Rollison's hat and cane.

'Patton,' Rollison said, 'one day you'll outgrow your halo.'

He had the satisfaction of putting Patton momentarily out of countenance. Then Lady Gloria came hobbling energetically on her stick from a room next to the drawing-room.

'I hope you can stop this absurd altercation,'

114

she said without preamble. 'I've tried once, but I will not go in again. I should have ordered them out of the house, but I knew you wanted to see them. Richard, what *is* it all about?'

'One hundred and forty-four tins of tainted salmon started it,' said Rollison. 'If you want to blame anyone, blame Aunt Matilda. How is she today?'

'Don't ask irrelevant questions. Go in and quell that riot.' Lady Gloria pointed her stick towards the door, and as Rollison turned, added: 'Mattie's much better.'

He did not tap before entering, but opened the door swiftly. Angela Gerrard was standing sideways towards him, in front of the fireplace but half-way into the room. Farther back was a tall young man in morning clothes. He looked hot and flustered, partly because he was considerably too fat for a man in the twenties.

'If you don't stop shouting—' began Angela.

'I'm not shouting—you are! I would never have believed it of you.'

'If you say that again I'll scream!'

'I hope it will be a hearty scream,' said Rollison gently.

They turned in movements so quick and identical that they appeared to be operated by a single pivot. The man's face dropped, and the girl paused. Her face was flushed and her eyes angry—even more angry than when she had been with him in the taxi.

'Did you or did you not take my wallet?'

115

she demanded.

'I certainly did,' confessed Rollison.

'There you are,' snapped Angela, swinging round on the young man. 'Now perhaps you'll believe me.'

Her suitor ignored her.

He had rather small blue eyes, wide open and staring almost incredulously at the Toff. He might have been frightened, or alarmed, or simply eager.

'Did you really?' His voice was taut.

'Do I have to repeat myself?' asked Rollison. 'I did, and I have it with me. Sit down, Angela, but introduce us first.'

'I want that wallet,' declared the young man aggressively.

'You can't have it. It's Angela's.'

'There are some things of mine in it! She had no right to let you have it. Give it to me!' He held out his hand, pale, plump and damp.

Rollison eyed the girl.

'Who is he, Angela?'

'That proves it!' shouted the young man, swinging round to the girl. 'You've been lying to me all along. You said you'd never seen him until this morning, but he calls you Angela. This finishes me. Give me that wallet, and I'll clear out.'

'Angela,' said Rollison patiently, 'what is the young man's name?'

'My name's Abbott, but that doesn't matter,' roared the man.

Angela looked from Abbott to Rollison, drew a deep breath, and then said with a deliberation which amused Rollison:

'Mr Rollison, this is Mr Frederick Abbott.' She paused. 'We were once engaged.'

'A lucky escape,' murmured Rollison.

'Will you two stop talking and give me my wallet?' shrieked Abbott. 'I won't stand here another minute!' He paused, then turned sharply to Angela. 'What do you mean—"*once engaged*"? We are now; I haven't released you.'

'I've sacked *you*,' said Angela scathingly.

'Don't talk nonsense! Just because you've lost your temper there's no need to make a fool of yourself.'

Angela bit her underlip.

Rollison unbuttoned a pocket of his tunic and, with Freddy Abbott now giving him his full attention, took out the notecase. For a moment he had wondered whether Jolly had replaced it, but it was there, untouched.

Abbott stretched forward.

'That's it; I'll have it.'

The speed of Abbott's grab took him by surprise, and it changed hands. Angela gasped again. Freddy backed, perhaps because he was suddenly aware of the grimness of Rollison's expression.

Then he turned and ran towards the open window, reached it, and began to clamber through. Once there had been iron railings between the house and the pavement, but they

117

had been removed for war scrap, and it was easy to get to the street.

Rollison paused to get his balance, and when only Abbott's right leg remained in the room, reached him and grabbed his ankle. Abbott tried to kick, but was in too precarious a position. Instead he lost his balance, crying out as he fell.

No one was passing 7 Braddon Place at the moment, for which the Toff was grateful. Retaining a grip on Abbott's leg he followed him through the window. The fall had dazed the fat man, who did not resist when Rollison hauled him to his feet, then lifted him and pushed him feet first through the window.

Abbott staggered and nearly fell, but Angela was close enough to save him.

Clutched in his right hand was the wallet.

Angela took it quickly.

'My turn, I think,' said Rollison politely, and promptly relieved her of it. 'Don't look daggers at me, Angela, I'm a much nicer chap than your ex-fiance. What on earth were you thinking about?'

Angela stared at him.

Tight-lipped and bright-eyed, she looked enchanting, for she had more natural colour than rouge and the sparkle in her eyes was glorious. For perhaps ten seconds they eyed each other, with Abbott gasping and groaning on the arm of a chair.

Then Angela began to laugh.

118

At first Rollison had an unpleasant suspicion that she was going to cry, her face was so distorted. Then he realized that she was laughing. The door opened then, and Lady Gloria put her head in.

'Are you all right in here?'

'We're doing fine!' Rollison assured her quickly. 'Shoo!'

The head was withdrawn and the door closed with a click. Rollison went to the window and lowered it enough to make sure that Abbott could not get out if he made another wild dash, went to an occasional table, and placed the notecase on it. He looked across at Angela, who approached him purposefully.

'Feeling better?' inquired Rollison solicitously. 'Things strike you like that sometimes, don't they? Is there anything here you particularly don't want me to see?'

'No-o. But—'

'You don't see why I should see any of it? Nor do I,' admitted Rollison. 'But I'm curious about Freddy's anxiety to get his possessions back. Which was his particular fancy, do you know?'

'That envelope,' said Angela, pointing to a sealed one which came out of a partition marked 'lb.' 'I don't—oh, it doesn't matter; you'll only find a few photographs and some money.'

'I hope losing the money didn't run you short,' said Rollison.

119

He put Abbott's letter aside, then glanced at the other contents, determined to make sure that Angela did not deceive him. Photographs, three pound notes and two ten-shilling ones, some postage stamps and a little book of National Savings stamps were the sole contents. He glanced at the photographs. There were six snapshots in all, three of Angela and Freddy Abbott together, one each of Angela and Freddy alone, and a sixth of a much older man. All had for background a garden and a large Georgian house. Rollison studied one deliberately, while Angela stood by his side.

Rollison looked up,

'He's like you, Angela,' he said quietly.

'Yes.' Her voice was dry. 'It's my father.'

'I thought perhaps he was,' said Rollison, glancing at Abbott. He raised his voice a little, and went on: 'I saw Barbicue after you'd gone, and he told me of a grievance and what he called your illusion. He thought you shot at him because you believed he had killed your father, or was to blame for his suicide.'

'It *was* his fault,' said Angela slowly. 'But I didn't shoot him.'

'Good. Don't try to again,' said Rollison. 'If you succeed it will be murder, and you'll be hanged—or at best detained during the King's pleasure.'

'I didn't *try* to shoot him,' insisted Angela tensely. 'I've never fired a gun in my life.'

Rollison eyed her intently, and for the first

120

time began to believe her.

'If you didn't we'll have to find out who did,' he remarked. 'I'm most anxious to know what reasons you have for thinking Barbicue swindled your father, too. Before that perhaps I ought to tell you what I'm trying to do, but I'm not sure that I want Mr Abbott to know. I have taken an acute dislike to the gentleman,' he added, stepping towards Frederick Abbott and staring down at him.

'I don't give a damn what you've taken,' said Abbott, coming to life, 'except my papers. Give them to me!'

'When I've read them,' said the Toff.

'You're not going to read them; I won't let you! What the hell do you think you're doing? I'll send for the police if you don't hand them over at once.'

'All right, send for the police,' said Rollison, obligingly.

He was trying to understand the fear which showed in the man's eyes, and its causes; and he wanted to make him angry enough to explain his desperate anxiety to regain the envelope.

Angela was watching her ex-fiance as closely, and consequently neither of them heard the door open. Abbott could not see the door because Rollison was in his way.

'Stay where you are!' said a man quietly.

Rollison stood quite still, except for turning his head. Angela gasped and turned in a flurry, while Abbott straightened up in his chair and stared towards the door.

Rollison did not recognize the man, but a child would have known that the revolver in his hand was no plaything. What Rollison noticed more particularly than the gun was the absence of a silencer.

'Don't be fool enough to move, Rollison,' said the man with the gun. 'Hurry up, David!'

Past him came Barbicue's David of the high forehead, his round face set in anxious apprehension. He tip-toed towards the table and picked up the envelope, then turned and went rabbit-like towards the door. Rollison took a half-step forward.

'I don't want to shoot you,' the gunman said.

'You don't want to make a noise, you mean,' Rollison retorted.

He was too far away to make a rush, and unless he stayed where he was the other would probably shoot.

David disappeared.

The gunman waited for perhaps ten seconds. David went out of the front door and hurried along the pavement, passing the window in their sight. Not until then did the gunman back to the door, slipping out and closing it behind him.

Rollison sprang to the window.

CHAPTER TWELVE

A COLLISION AND SOME CURSES

Rollison had the window up again and his revolver ready, but the gunman did not leave by the front door.

Abbott shouted in a high-pitched voice:

'Get my letter; get it back!'

'In good time, yes,' said Rollison.

He climbed out of the window and ran along the pavement. Halfway along Braddon Place there was a service alley, and he guessed that his man had gone that way, using the rear entrance of the house. There was a chance of catching him, if a slim one.

He was running by the time he reached the entrance to the alley, but was in time to see the gunman take a running leap into a small open car. At the wheel was David, peering anxiously over his shoulder.

Whatever David's other qualifications, he knew how to drive. He sent the car zigzagging for the first ten yards, avoiding the two shots Rollison sent towards him. Then the car turned a corner, and was presented broadside-on. Rollison fired again. As he did so he stumbled, for someone cannoned into him and then reeled back against the wall of the corner house.

'Oh, *damn* you!' cursed Abbott.

'The same to you,' said the Toff, and for a moment was in the grip of a cold fury.

Abbott saw the expression in his eyes and tried to back into the wall. They stood quite still for perhaps five seconds, then hurrying footsteps drew near and Rollison turned away abruptly. There was no point in letting his rage get the better of him.

A policeman drew up.

'Who did that shooting?' He was breathless, and obviously impartial, since the gun was in Rollison's hand.

'I did,' said Rollison. 'Constable, I want...' He paused and then said hastily: 'Come to Number Seven, will you, and bring that with you.'

He indicated Abbott with the scathing 'that', and before the constable could try to stop him hurried back to the house.

On the threshold stood Angela, by her side Lady Gloria and Patton. Patton was blue with fright, and Glory was saying tartly:

'What is the matter with you? You're not hurt, are you?'

'No-n-no,' stuttered Patton. 'B-but—'

Rollison went into the drawing-room, lifted the telephone and dialled Whitehall 1212.

While he waited for the connection there were other sounds in the hall and the room. The constable, Abbott, Glory and Angela entered, all coming to a stop when they saw

124

what he was doing.

'Scotland Yard; can I help you?' a voice intoned.

'Superintendent Grice, please,' said Rollison, and gave his name. Grice was at the other end in a few seconds, saying at once that he was glad to hear from Rollison.

'It's almost accidental,' admitted Rollison. 'Will you get a call out at once for a two-seater M.G., number CJ—. Are you putting this down?'

'Yes,' said Grice.

'CJ21J,' continued the Toff. 'Dark blue or black; last seen going from Braddon Place in the Oxford Street direction. Driver a thin man with a big head—turnip-head if you like—fair hair, light-grey suit, answers to "David". Am I going too fast?'

'No.'

'Passenger a male about five-feet ten, dressed in dark brown, regular features, brown hair, brown trilby hat with a coloured feather in the band, right side. Nasal voice, but no particular accent; name not known, but carrying a gun, probably a Webley .32.'

'What are they wanted for?' demanded Grice.

'Robbery, and uttering threats,' said Rollison on the spur of the moment. 'And Grice. The "David" is an assistant to Justin Barbicue and staying at the Splendide Hotel. I'm going to see Barbicue myself, but you might want to keep an eye on the hotel in case his "David" heads that way.'

'All right,' said Grice obligingly. 'Don't take too much on yourself, though.' That was a hope more than a command, perhaps only a concession to formality: Stoddart might care a great deal, but Grice cared little how bad men were caught.

Rollison replaced the receiver, then turned to find the others drawn in a semi-circle about him, Lady Gloria and Angela close together, the constable and Abbott next to them. Abbott's face was pale, and his lips were set tightly. The constable was fingering the steel helmet in his hand.

'Can you make a report out of what you heard?' Rollison asked him. 'It would save me valuable time.'

'That will be all right, sir, yes.' Clearly Rollison's talk with Grice had impressed the policeman.

'You might ask the butler for additional data on how the gunman got in here. Thanks, constable.' Rollison smiled as the man went out, then looked at Glory, hesitating before saying: 'Aunt Gloria, could you and Miss Gerrard find something in common for ten minutes?'

'I should have expected that,' said Glory, and set her lips. 'Come along, Angela.'

Angela hesitated, but followed her out of the room.

126

Rollison put his right hand deep into his pocket and regarded Abbott with acute distaste. Abbott was clenching and unclenching his hands.

'What are you looking at me like that for? It wasn't my fault. If you'd given me the envelope before, I would have been away and there wouldn't have been any trouble. You did it, you fool; it's no use blaming me.'

'I wouldn't blame you if you walked in front of a bus as soon as you left here,' said Rollison icily. 'Nor would I mourn for you. If you'd had the sense to stay where you were we would have had the letter and the men. What was in it?'

'That's my business!'

'And mine—and Scotland Yard's.'

'It's nothing to do with any of you, and no one can make me say what was in it. I know my rights.' Abbott gulped. 'If you must know, there were a thousand pounds. A thousand pounds in Bank of England notes—my money!' His voice rose to a screech. 'You've lost it, you've let it go! I'll sue you for the money! I'll go straight to my solicitor and sue you for it!'

'What were you doing with a thousand pounds?' asked Rollison.

'That's my business, too! I—I'd just sold—sold a house.'

Abbott gulped again, and there were actually tears in his small blue eyes. 'I've been trying to get that money for six months, and

127

now when I get it that happens! I'll see you pay up!'

'You sold a house to Barbicue,' said Rollison thoughtfully, 'and Barbicue's clerk comes after you. That might be true.'

'What do you mean—it might be? It is! Are you calling me a liar?'

'I couldn't put my tongue on words to describe you,' said the Toff. 'Go to your lawyer if you want, but before then you'll give me evidence, with dotted "i's" and crossed "t's", that you had a house and sold it to Barbicue.'

'I won't stand any more of these insults!'

'You'll stand plenty,' said Rollison. He took a diary from his pocket, tore out a page and wrote on it, then pressed a bell. After a pause, a middle-aged maid entered; Patton was either still helpless with fright or being questioned by the constable.

'Take this to Lady Gloria at once,' said Rollison.

'Yes, sir.' The maid took the note and went out as Abbott demanded explosively:

'What was that?'

'Is that your business, too?' Rollison took cigarettes from his pocket and proffered them. 'I suppose you have some of the human vices, you're not all righteous.' Abbott's hand was unsteady as he took a cigarette between forefinger and thumb heavily stained with nicotine. 'Now sit down and try to talk and act normally.'

Abbott sat down, and after a little persuasion talked to the Toff. The house, he declared, was a small one in Fulham. It was damaged from bombing, otherwise he would have asked more than a thousand pounds. Yes, he had sold it to Barbicue, who had paid him in cash that morning.

'Why cash?' asked Rollison.

'I—I preferred it that way,' said Abbott. 'I don't trust Barbicue, not after—' He paused.

'After what?' encouraged the Toff.

Then the story broke; it did not surprise Rollison for it fitted well into the background, and there was enough to suggest that Abbott was telling the truth.

Abbott had been Gerrard's secretary, and had lost his job when Gerrard had died; it had been a well-paid one. Although he had never been charged, there was suspicion against him in the business circles in which he had moved, and he had not been able to get another really remunerative post. He had a C3 heart; that was why he was not in the Army. He had heavy financial commitments, and had soon spent his savings. The only realizable asset in his possession had been the house in Fulham, and he had known that Barbicue was paying cash for London suburban property. Because he had not trusted Barbicue, whom he believed had really been behind Gerrard's failure, he had insisted on payment in cash.

Had Abbott known that Angela was staying

129

at the 'Splendide'?

'Of course I knew,' said Abbott. 'We're engaged, aren't we? I don't see why she had to stay there; she could have come to my flat, but she wouldn't. She was damned particular about the room she had, too.'

'Yes?' Rollison made the word a question.

'Look here, what about my money?'

'The police will probably pick David up within twenty-four hours,' said Rollison. 'Worry about that later.'

'That's all very well, but—'

Rollison managed to reassure him without losing too much time and Abbott left the house. Rollison watched him walking past the window, and a second afterwards Jolly passed on the other side of the road.

Rollison was smiling when the door opened and Lady Gloria and Angela entered.

'So you phoned, like a good Aunt,' approved Rollison.

'I suppose there is some sense in your absurd requests,' said Lady Gloria acidly. 'You asked me to telephone Jolly and tell him to come here and then follow Abbott, and I did. Let me tell *you*, Richard, that I did not need your description of Abbott; I am quite capable of passing on a description without your guidance.'

'Why did you do it?' demanded Angela.

Rollison stepped to a chair and sat on its arm, suddenly very tired.

'Glory,' he said soberly, 'don't be aggressive. I know it relieves your feelings, but not just now, please. Later, as much and as often as you like.'

Gloria stared at him, and her face relaxed.

'Upon my soul!' she said. 'I think you ought to have a cup of tea. Bless the boy,' she added *sotto voce*, 'he must be tired out.'

The door closed behind her, and Angela Gerrard approached Rollison slowly and quietly. She stood looking at him, her face not two feet from his, vivid in the youth that was hers, yet just then looking in some queer way mature; her expression was not unlike Glory's.

'Would you prefer to talk to me later?' she asked quietly.

Rollison smiled up at her, much of his sudden weariness easing. He was at a loss to explain why Lady Gloria's acid remark had affected him so much, but knew that he would welcome some tea.

'No, now, Angela. Sit down—and take this as an apology, I haven't been as nice as I should be. There hasn't been time,' he added defensively. 'I suppose I am trying to grope in too much darkness for too many things, but at least they link up at occasional intervals.'

'Do they?'

'Yes. I've told you what I understand from Barbicue. You're convinced that he was behind your father's failure, aren't you?'

'There's no doubt at all, in my mind. Don't

131

ask me for evidence, though, the only man who could have helped lied when I went to the police. Oh, I suppose I couldn't expect them to take any notice of me, but—'

'Who was the man?' asked Rollison.

'Father's manager. It was a brokerage company, and Lett handled as much of the work as Father.'

Rollison stared at her with a quickening interest.

'That is the name? *Lett!*'

'Yes.' If Angela was puzzled by his manner she did not say so, but went on: 'I thought Lett could have proved that the affairs got into the mess when Barbicue was a partner. A lot of clients' money was involved, and I *know* Barbicue took it. I—I feel it,' she added a little wildly, 'and Father knew too, but he said there wasn't any proof. I believe Lett could have supplied the proof, but he said he knew it was Father. So—I had to stop worrying the police.'

Rollison said slowly: 'Edward Lett?'

'No, James.'

'Frequently dressed in black? Tall, scraggy?'

'You know him!' exclaimed Angela.

Rollison stood up, and was smiling much more happily. The Letts and the Barbicue connection with the Gerrards was the key factor, and needed concentration.

'We've met,' he admitted. 'And I think he's beginning to wish he hadn't lied. I think he would be much happier if Barbicue were in Jail.

Now—' he spoke more soberly: 'The truth and the whole truth. Did you shoot at Barbicue this morning?'

'No.' Angela's eyes were quite steady.

'How many people knew your room?'

She was startled. 'Two, I think. Freddy and Mr Bennison. Of course, others might have known.'

'Who is Bennison?'

'A family friend,' said Angela. 'He wouldn't have shot at Barbicue; that would be absurd. Nor would Freddy. It needn't have been anyone who knew where I was staying there, need it?'

'No,' admitted Rollison slowly. 'It could have been a man or woman who chose the room because it was opposite Barbicue's. Freddy told me that you made quite a fuss about getting that particular room. Why?'

Angela raised her hands, a helpless little gesture.

'Oh, it was silly of me, I suppose. But I knew Barbicue was staying there, and that he used the room as an office. I thought—I thought if I watched him I'd find out whether Lett went to see him. Lett always denied that he had any dealings with Barbicue, you see. I suppose I ought to have tried to put it out of my mind, but that's not as easy as it sounds. If you've ever hated anyone as I hate Barbicue you'd know what I mean.' She went to a chair and sat down. 'Except to Freddy, I've never talked

133

about it before. I've tried to sink myself in work, but something always happens to remind me. It's an obsession. You—you're practically the first man I've ever met who hasn't liked Barbicue.'

'Except for Freddy?' asked Rollison.

'Yes. Although I don't think he really feels much one way or the other.' She grimaced. 'I can't think why I ever said I'd marry him. Thank God I've kept putting the day off, and now—' She stared for a moment, and then laughed shortly. 'It's too funny, isn't it? I'm talking to you like a long-lost brother! Or'— she grew sober at once—'like Father. We—we were always such good friends,' she added slowly. 'I felt that while I didn't go on trying to clear his name I was letting him down.'

Rollison said quietly:

'You haven't let him down, Angela. Now let me have Bennison's address—and Freddy's, will you?'

Angela gave him the addresses as Lady Gloria entered with a tea-tray, although it was nearly seven o'clock. Rollison welcomed the tea, and Angela gave the impression that she had not had a drink for a week. Gloria eased the tension, also, by a description of Patton still in a 'blue funk'.

Rollison chuckled at this final condemnation of the butler, then looked at his watch. He stared down, and:

'Good Lord, that dinner!' He jumped up,

positively in a flurry, and reached the telephone in a few strides. He dialled Lane's number, to be told that Lane, of Lane, Shapley and Lane, had left for the Regal Hotel.

'What are you acting like a jackanapes for?' demanded Lady Gloria.

'Jack-in-the-box,' corrected Rollison distractedly. 'No dinner ordered, no interview with Barbicue. Glory, can you—can you go to the "Regal" and keep Andy Lane happy for an hour? Take Angela with you. You can have the best dinner in London while you're there. I'll phone Alphonse about it.'

'But—' began Glory.

'I can't—' started Angela.

'Both of you,' pleaded Rollison urgently. 'No one dresses for dinner now except the outmoded and the unfeeling, so that's no excuse. Tell Andy I was shot at, kicked at, laughed at—anything you like, but keep him there until I arrive.'

'Where are you going?' demanded Lady Gloria. 'Before I go gallivanting about I need to be sure that it's for something worthwhile.'

'I'm going to interview the seller of bad salmon,' declared Rollison. 'Glory, don't be obdurate for the sake of it. Angela's dying to go, you can see it in her eyes.' He turned from them to the telephone and dialled the 'Regal', while Glory and Angela exchanged glances, suggesting that they would soon get to know and like one another well. They went out of the room.

Alphonse came to the phone, heard, promised; naturally, he knew Mr Lane. He would have a word with Livy, too. For Mr Rollison, it was a pleasure.

Rollison hoped there would be some pleasure in interviewing Barbicue.

CHAPTER THIRTEEN

SAD FATE OF A TWO-SEATER

'Quite frankly, my dear Rollison,' boomed Barbicue, 'I find it impossible to believe you. I know that you have some peculiar ideas. I have known David for fifteen years. Fifteen *years*! He would do no such thing.'

'Too bad,' said Rollison. 'First your confidence, then your vanity, and finally your trust in mankind, all being undermined on the same day. You know the old saw about the higher you go the farther you fall? Here's another. The bigger you're inflated the louder the bang when you burst. You're about to burst.'

'This is intolerable,' snapped Barbicue. 'You are a subject for—'

'Psycho-analysis, like Angela?'

'Oh, I'll talk no more with you,' declared Barbicue.

'You'll talk with me,' said the Toff grimly. 'When the police arrest David he also will talk, and he'll tell the unpleasant story of how you sent him to follow Abbott to get the money back.'

'That he never will,' said Barbicue abruptly. 'The last time I saw David he was about to arrange for a parcel to be delivered to a friend.' Barbicue paused and fixed Rollison with his imperious gaze. 'He should have been back by four o'clock this afternoon, but failed to report. I have been perturbed by his continued absence, but I flatly refuse to believe that there is an atom of truth in this preposterous accusation.'

'The police know of it,' said Rollison.

'I shall tell them that you are lying.'

Rollison sat more comfortably on a corner of a table in the inner room of Barbicue's suite, and said reflectively:

'You're not the man I thought you were by a long way. Every once in a while a figure arises, an imitation Churchill of crime. I had hopes that you might be one, but you lie too badly. Did Abbott sell you a house?'

'He did. Perhaps you would like to see the deeds?' Barbicue descended to a sneer.

'I would,' said Rollison.

Barbicue stared in surprise, then made a decisive movement to one of the filing cabinets.

'Very good, Major Rollison. You *shall*.'

Rollison saw the deeds and the transfer,

137

noting that the solicitor who had handled the transaction was a Mr Raymond Bennison. He remembered Angela's mention of the man. He whistled a little as he made sure that the transfer was legal and duly stamped at Somerset House, then dropped the documents back on the filing cabinet, and mused:

'Barbicue, I'll give you some credit. You would not have sent David and the other hopeful to collect a thousand pounds just like that. Particularly not to Braddon Place, knowing that I was likely to be there.'

'That is just what I have been saying.'

'But you would if there was something else in the envelope, something which could serve as evidence against you. What was it?'

Barbicue clenched his right hand and banged it into the palm of his left.

'This morning I awakened to a sane world, to a period of difficulty and the perplexities of the day no doubt, but a sane, a practical world. Now I have received three visits from you, I have listened to your absurd vapourings too often. I am a rogue. I buy and sell goods illegally, I ruin that child's father, I turn my trusted clerk into a criminal, I kill a policeman, I set fire to public houses, I—'

'Poison my aunt's salmon,' interpolated the Toff.

'What!'

'My aunt's salmon,' said Rollison. 'There is a time in a life of crime when even master criminals make a fatal mistake. My aunt's salmon was yours.'

'You,' gasped Barbicue, 'you—you—'

'"Buffoon" was the last effort,' said Rollison amiably. 'No, that was mine, yours was "mountebank". Have a cigarette?'

'Get out of my sight!' shouted Barbicue.

Rollison lit a cigarette himself, and swung his legs.

'As you say, it's not been a nice day. The assault was too sudden and too well sustained. Thanks to James Lett, who cracked so badly, I learned of you—and I realized that I had to do just one thing. *Break* you, Barbicue. I am now an interested spectator of the fracture. The police are watching your suite, in case David should return.'

'That is a lie!'

'It is the sober truth,' said Rollison. 'I passed a sergeant outside. He may or may not know that you're the man responsible for Melsom's death but he'll learn quite soon, and then he will follow you to the ends of the earth, Barbicue, or the shores of England, which are as far as you'll get. There is an honour among policemen, and loyalty beyond your conception.'

'They would not be such half-wits as to believe you.' Barbicue was perspiring freely, not altogether because of the warmth; and a pleasant breeze was coming through the open window. 'Such fools,' emphasised Barbicue.

139

'Go and see for yourself,' invited Rollison.

Barbicue made a sound which was like *pfui*! and took a cigar case from his waistcoat pocket. He lit a cigar and flicked the match across the room. It struck against the bottom of the window, and bounced back.

Before either of them spoke there was a tap at the door.

Barbicue started. Rollison watched him narrowly, and waited while he went to the door. His hand was unsteady as he pulled back the bolt, then turned the handle.

Rollison sat up more erect, for Grice in person was standing on the threshold.

'Good evening,' said Barbicue, and waved his cigar.

'Good evening,' said Grice. 'I am an officer from Scotland Yard.' He proffered his card, and Barbicue glanced down at it as he clutched the door, quite tensely. Rollison doubted whether he read the card.

'Er—what can I do for you, sir?' Barbicue's voice was taut.

'Read, Barbicue, read,' murmured Rollison. 'Your caller's name is Grice—Superintendent Grice. He is going to put all the little men and the big men who go to market into jail. Aren't you, Superintendent?'

Grice showed no surprise at seeing him, but stepped past Barbicue into the room. There was a gleam of understanding in his eyes, an unspoken promise not to take the edge off

Rollison's assault. Barbicue closed the door and, breathing heavily, asked why he had been honoured with a visit.

'I doubt if they've come to arrest you yet,' said the Toff. 'They will before long.'

'On what charge?' inquired Grice.

It was just the touch needed to make Barbicue gulp and step towards a cupboard, from which he took a bottle of whisky and some glasses. He retained his composure well enough to offer them a drink; both refused. He poured himself a long one.

'Superintendent,' he said when he had recovered. 'I wish to make a complaint. This man has pestered me throughout the day, making absurd accusations which have not the flimsiest of foundations. I wish to have him removed from my rooms.'

'Is this true, Major Rollison?' asked Grice expressionlessly.

Rollison laughed.

'I came to tell him about his clerk, and he appears to think that I'm accusing him of sending his clerk to rob Freddy Abbott.'

Barbicue stared at him, round-eyed.

'I hope that I did misread your innuendo, Major Rollison,' he said stiffly. 'I think perhaps in the heat of the moment I read more in the Major's words than was intended Mr— Superintendent.' He looked at the card, lying on the cabinet, and nodded. 'Now, sir, what can I do for you?'

Grice appeared to be quite satisfied, and said quietly:

'You employ a man named Bliss—David Bliss, Mr Barbicue?'

'That is so. Let me say at this juncture that I cannot believe that David would do any such thing as Mr Rollison appears to imagine.'

'I understand that there is satisfactory evidence to support Major Rollison's statement,' said Grice pedantically. 'Did Bliss own an M.G. sports car numbered CJ21J?'

'I cannot remember the number, sir, but he had such a car, yes. I was always alarmed at the speed with which he considered it necessary to drive. I believe that there should be a much stricter speed limit, and—'

'Bliss and the car crashed on the Epping Road, on the other side of Loughton,' said Grice, sharply. The statement seemed callous, almost brutal. 'Bliss was killed outright, and the car is almost unrecognizable.'

Barbicue stood swaying on his feet.

'Good—*God*!' he gasped. 'Good—*God*! David!' He goggled at Grice, then smoothed his forehead, swallowed hard and turned again to the whisky.

Yet Rollison noticed that his hand was quite steady now. Not all the time, for it shook as he moved for the bottle, but nothing spilled; the actual task of pouring was successfully accomplished.

'I can hardly believe it,' Barbicue said in a

142

low voice. 'That boy has worked for me for fifteen years.'

'There's too big a strain on your credulity,' said Rollison. 'There is nothing at all you believe.'

'Do you mind, Major Rollison?' Grice wanted him silent. 'There is little doubt that the smash was caused deliberately; the steering-gear had been tampered with.'

'No! No, I—'

'—Can't believe it,' said Rollison, finding the remark irresistible. 'Sorry, Superintendent.'

Barbicue swung round on him.

The man's face was livid and his eyes were glaring. He raised a fist and looked about to use it. He used every adjective, mostly obscene, that could describe Rollison or his children or his antecedents. Coming after his wordy pomposity and precise phraseology, there was a nauseating beastliness about his outburst. Not until he had raved for several minutes did he seem to appreciate that he was not creating a good impression on Grice. He quietened down.

'Such an exhibition of callous indifference in the face of the brutal death of a young man, a dear friend of mine, I have never thought it likely to experience. I am appalled by you, Major. *Appalled.*'

Grice stood quite still as Rollison eyed the big man with half-closed eyes, and said:

'I'm not even mildly surprised by you, Mr

143

Barbicue. Good night. I'll see you in the foyer, shall I, Superintendent?'

Grice nodded.

Barbicue made a hissing sound between his lips as he watched Rollison leave.

Ten minutes after Rollison had reached the foyer, Grice emerged from one of the lifts. He was smiling a little as he approached Rollison and they walked into the street.

'How did you know that Barbicue was our man?' he demanded.

'Do we know?' countered Rollison.

'On that showing, yes. The man is scared out of his wits. What have you done to him?'

Rollison chuckled.

'Talked. And talked and talked. We won't go into details, but I heard a story which suggested he might be in it, and I sailed in with all fours. He hasn't really recovered from the first shock, and I've been at him all the time. You came just at the right moment,' he added appreciatively. 'He was thinking of demanding to see his solicitor, and picturing himself in the dock, I think. You've nothing against him, have you?'

'Nothing at all,' admitted Grice. 'We've thought he needed watching occasionally, since—'

'The Gerrard case?'

Grice shot him a sidelong glance.

'So you're on to that?' He raised a hand as if in wonderment, and went on: 'Yes. He went

144

close to the borderline once or twice after the Government Order preventing the traffic in plots of land where property had been blitzed, but he was always just on the right side. Now he's buying more and more property: some good, some bad. It's a gamble which may be justified. Land values will go up, but they may not go as far as he seems to think.'

'Have you ever asked yourself where he gets his money?'

'I am doing, now.'

'And we don't need to look far,' said the Toff. 'From the "market", Grice, from the "market". He must have an organization quite huge in size; he must be making hundreds of thousands.'

'Probably,' said Grice, and then laughed somewhat ruefully. 'You have an uncanny ability to get right at the—' He paused.

'Jolly suggested "fountain-head",' murmured the Toff.

'Yes. Haven't you?'

'I was pushed, this time. One day, when you're no longer a policeman, I'll tell you how it happened. Meanwhile there's another man you want badly. One James Lett, brother of your Edward.' He paused, but as Grice said nothing he went on: 'This Lett, my Lett, was general manager of Gerrard's.'

'I've just been thinking,' said Grice. 'His daughter—Gerrard's daughter—came to see us, blaming Barbicue for the crash. I wasn't at

145

the Yard then, I was at B2, but I've been reading the case up. Gerrard was suspected of black-market selling, but there was no evidence of it when he died, and we had full access to his papers. It looked as if we were wrong. If Barbicue was really behind that, he could have been the—'

'Black marketeer,' said Rollison.

'What an amazing fellow you are!' exclaimed Grice, and did not enlarge. 'Barbicue could have taken all records of the trading, as well as anything which incriminated him. The daughter said that this man Lett could give the necessary evidence, but Lett corroborated Barbicue.'

'So she's told me.'

'Who? The Gerrard girl?' Grice was startled. 'How did you find her?'

'We met,' said Rollison airily. 'You'll have Barbicue watched now, of course?'

'Yes. Mind you, we can't be sure, yet.'

'Tell your men to be careful,' said Rollison. 'We don't want more accidents like Melsom's, although I think we can say he died in a good cause. It's astonishing how many ways there are of dying in this war, isn't it?' After a moment's sombre pause he went on: 'Look here: I've a dinner date. Will you come along to the "Regal" with me and have a snack? Also a talk with Andrew Lane? He's going to give me the histories of Barbicue and Gerrard.'

Grice looked regretful.

'I've too much to do,' he said. 'What I'd like before the night is out is another talk with you. I suspect that you're keeping a lot to yourself.'

'What time will you be leaving the Yard?'

'In time for breakfast if this goes on,' Grice said with a grimace. 'I need more reports about Bliss's death. I want to talk to Edward Lett. And now there's this call out for his brother. I suppose you can justify it if we get him?'

'Yes. And he'll justify you getting Barbicue,' said Rollison confidently.

Grice said slowly: 'Are you so sure?'

'Reasonably sure,' said the Toff, 'if he lives long enough. Barbicue knows that James Lett betrayed him, and I think he'll try to do for James. I gather,' he added, 'that James in turn will fight shy of Barbicue, but whether he can is another matter. You'll concentrate on the Epping district, won't you?'

Grice nodded. 'Yes. So you're not keeping much to yourself?' He laughed drily. 'You've learned nothing about Epping except that the one Lett was going there, and that Bliss was killed on that road, I suppose?'

'Nothing at all,' Rollison told him truthfully.

Soon, he strolled towards the 'Regal'. It was comforting and reassuring to know that Grice was prepared, discreetly, to condone the irregularities of his procedure. He had worked too often with the police obstructing him in one way, and their mutual adversary

147

in another.

There were many things he could have discussed with Grice, and one in particular weighed heavily on his mind, the method by which Barbicue contrived his buying and selling. The organization must be considerable, and his agents many. As he walked Rollison decided that there was no need to worry about that then; when Barbicue finally cracked, the rest of the dark edifice would crumble.

On reaching the hotel he went to the dining-room. There was music and dancing, and the room was crowded. He could not see Angela, Glory, or Lane, and he frowned as he contemplated the corner table which Alphonse had promised him—he had chosen a corner because he wanted to talk more or less in confidence to Lane. He continued to frown until Alphonse came bearing down on him, enormous in his black and white, with a pointed French beard and waxed moustaches, both jet black.

'Why, M'sieu, I am so sorry you were not able to come, but the others, I assure you, they 'ad all they require. An' more.' Alphonse waited for praise, was disappointed, and added: 'There is something more you need, M'sieu? They were dissatisfied? I cannot believe it. I will not believe it.' He struck an attitude. 'M'sieu, the worst; I beg of you to tell me the worst.'

Rollison said with an effort:

'No, you tell me. Where are they?'

'M'sieu, the expression in your eyes, it worries me. Please, what is it which gave cause for dissatisfaction?'

'Alphonse,' said Rollison urgently, 'where are they? I was to join them here.'

'But, M'sieu, you are ill!' declared Alphonse roundly. 'They come, they eat, they drink, they 'ave *every*t'ing everyt'ing which they cannot 'ave, you ask them. You send a word, a telephone and off they go before coffee, although for M'sieu Lane a Benedictine was waiting.'

'Where did they go?' said Rollison, and clenched a fist. 'Did they say where?'

'Yes, M'sieu, of course. To your flat. M'sieu, you sent that message. Please to understand, the message came.'

'The flat,' said Rollison. 'I wonder.' He smiled bleakly. 'Not your fault, Alphonse; you've done wonders. But I didn't send for them. Someone else did.'

'But who else would call them from your flat?'

'That's the first question,' said Rollison over his shoulder. 'And did they get there? is the second.'

149

CHAPTER FOURTEEN

'NO JOKE,' SAYS GLORY

It took Rollison ten minutes to reach the flat. His anxiety increased with each one, and he was sitting on the edge of the taxi seat most of the way. He had no thought of anything else in his mind but the message which had been falsely sent and trustfully taken. He did not think that it could be a trap for Glory or Lane; the idea hardly occurred to him. But he was suddenly and vividly aware that Angela Gerrard might be in danger.

'Wait,' he said to the taxi-driver, and hurried to the front door, up the stairs, and to his own landing. His door was closed, and although by then the evening was growing dark there was no light underneath it. He put the key in the lock, threw the door open, and stepped in swiftly.

He pulled up abruptly on the threshold.

Angela was there. She was sitting in the lounge opposite Lady Gloria. Standing by an open bookcase with a slim volume in his hand was Andrew Lane, short, sturdy, and grey. From the kitchen came sounds suggesting that coffee was being prepared.

Angela jumped from her chair as Rollison closed the door, Gloria glared up, and Lane continued to look at the book. Little short of a cataclysm would make Lane put aside a book until he had finished the paragraph he was reading; it had taken Rollison some time to realize that his imperturbability in that and other things was more than a pose.

'Richard,' said Gloria in a voice like a gathering storm, 'you may think differently, but this is no joke. Andrew, put that book down and talk to Richard.'

'A moment, Lady Gloria,' said Lane, without turning his head.

'Rolly!' exclaimed Angela, proving that she had discussed him with Gloria, and that Gloria had been free with the diminutive used when he was in favour. 'Where have you been? Why did you send for us? Is he mixed up in it? Did you expect the attack?'

The only question which really made an impression on him was: 'Did you expect the attack?'

'No,' he said slowly, 'I didn't expect anything, least of all this.'

Lane closed the book and turned deliberately, a man of slow movement, a ruddy complexion at variance with his manner, a broken nose certainly not typical of the legal profession, and a thick, close-cut moustache covering the whole of his upper lip and even drooping a little below the corners.

'I enjoyed dinner before we were hurried away,' he said mildly. 'What was the trouble, Rolly?'

151

Gloria made an explosive sound.

Rollison drew on his cigarette, and plunged into a vivid account of his feelings and reactions during the past twenty minutes. The effect was considerable, particularly on Lady Gloria, who had the un-Victorian habit of freely admitting when she was wrong.

'So you didn't send for us—the attack was meant for *you*,' she said.

'Now if I could hear about the attack I might feel better,' said Rollison. 'Is anybody hurt?'

'Yes. Freddy is,' said Angela.

'Freddy,' repeated Rollison blankly, and looked at the kitchen door. 'It would help if I knew just what happened, and how,' he added, and sat down.

Jolly came in with coffee; Jolly always seemed to be carrying a tray. He set it on a small table near Gloria and went back to the kitchen, leaving the door ajar so that he should miss none of the recital. The two women looked at Lane, who pursed his lips reflectively, sat down, and began to talk.

'We had been at the "Regal" for three-quarters of an hour, Rolly, when the message purporting to come from you was delivered.' He paused and smoothed his moustache. 'We thought you had asked us to hurry here, and left in the middle of savoury. Gloria always enjoys her savoury,' he added drily. 'We were here in a little over twenty minutes. Perhaps I

152

should say we were downstairs then. A young man—named Abbott, I understand—was waiting here, and joined us. Apparently he wanted to see you.'

Lane paused and smoothed his moustache again.

'A man passed us on a motor-cycle, or I should say drew near us,' Lane went on. 'He swerved his machine, stopped, and stabbed at young Abbott with a long-bladed knife. Then off he went; those machines make such an infernal clatter. It was growing dusk, and we could not see the man. That is all, except what is probably the most important thing. Jolly materialized and pushed Abbott out of the way of the knife. Otherwise I think the wound would have been much more severe than it was.'

Again Rollison looked at the kitchen door.

'Is Abbott badly hurt?'

'There is a nasty wound in his shoulder, and he lost consciousness,' said Lane. 'Jolly and Lady Gloria dressed it, and he is resting in your spare bedroom. I am a little concerned in case he is suffering from severe shock.'

'Nonsense,' snapped Lady Gloria. 'He's suffering from blue funk quite as bad as Patton's.' She handed coffee to Angela, Rollison taking Lane's and his own, and eyed her nephew. 'Do you think it was intended for an attack on you?'

'It could have been,' Rollison admitted. He

153

raised his voice. 'Jolly, come in a moment, will you?'

Jolly appeared with almost suspicious promptness.

'Where were you?' asked the Toff. 'And what did you see?'

'Mr Lane has described the incident perfectly, sir,' said Jolly. 'As you instructed, I had been following Abbott, and when he came here and called at the flat, finding no answer and waiting outside, I thought it best to wait also. I was in the porch next door, and both heard and saw the motor-cyclist. He was carrying the knife in his hand while holding the handlebars, and I saw it in time, moving very quickly in consequence. I was just a little too late to do more than hustle Mr Abbott and Miss Gerrard out of the way. They were backing on the roadway, and in the greater danger.'

'If you could see a knife there wasn't much likelihood that it was a mistake in identity,' mused Rollison.

'I don't think so,' admitted Jolly.

'So Abbott was deliberately attacked,' chimed in Lady Gloria.

Angela said: 'I wish I knew why he was in danger, Richard. Can you make head or tail of it?'

'Not yet,' admitted Rollison, and smiled one-sidedly. 'I'll see Freddy, he may decide to open his heart. Thanks, Jolly.' He exchanged glances with his man, and knew that Jolly shared his opinion of the attack, although both were unspoken. 'Come into Abbott's room with me, will you?'

'Very good, sir.'

Rollison looked at Abbott, who was wearing the jacket of a pair of his pyjamas, but appeared to have only one arm. He was awake, and staring at them narrow-eyed. His face was bloodless, and his plump cheeks sagged.

'Well, what?' asked Rollison.

'I think there is little doubt that the attack was intended for Miss Gerrard, sir,' said Jolly in a voice so low that even Abbott could not hear. 'She was nearer the motor-cyclist. I could only push Abbott forward, and against her. I have not, of course, disclosed that opinion to the others.'

'I don't think we will, yet. It fits in with the rest of what we know, Jolly. Someone phoned for them, and watched them arrive. The motor-cycle made a lot of noise, according to Mr Lane. Did it?'

'I heard the two-stroke engine start from round the corner; that was why I hurried, sir, and paid such particular attention.'

'How long did Abbott detain them?'

'Not more than a moment or two,' said Jolly decisively. 'As an opinion, sir, purely an opinion, I think that the cyclist would have had ample time, and been able to be much more selective, had he pulled up and followed them

155

into the house. They would not have been prepared for there was no reason for them to suspect such an attack.'

'So Abbott being there was providential,' mused the Toff. 'Partly because he delayed them, more especially because he brought you. Where has he been?'

'He went to his house in Fulham, sir, and then to his flat in Bayswater.'

'What kind of a flat is it?'

'I would say an expensive one,' Jolly reported. 'While he was at home I took the opportunity to make a number of inquiries. He has not the best of reputations, sir, and I think I can presume far enough to say that Miss Gerrard was very well advised to break off the engagement.'

Rollison frowned, 'How did you know about that?'

'Abbott was telling another man who visited him, a Mr Bennison.' He paused to allow the name to register, and the Toff reflected that Bennison had known that Barbicue was at the 'Splendide', and also that Angela's room was directly opposite his. 'Bennison is a frequent caller,' Jolly continued. 'I gathered that, and got his name from the housekeeper of another flat on the same floor. Later I followed them and heard much of their conversation. I gained the impression that Abbott was worried and indignant, more angry perhaps than indignant, but he gave no explanation of his anxiety.

156

Bennison is a smooth character, if I may put it so loosely, and tried to reassure him. This discussion took place over an evening meal, and Bennison left the restaurant about half past seven. Abbott came straight here.'

'Bennison; Bennison. Much depends on Bennison,' said the Toff. 'Have you discovered anything else about him?'

'I am afraid I have had neither time nor opportunity,' said Jolly. 'I have wondered whether that should be the next thing for me to do.'

'Do you know his address?'

'There are several Bennisons in the phone book, and I am not sure which is his.'

'Ask Miss Gerrard for it, I've forgotten,' said Rollison. He rested a hand on the other's shoulder. 'You'll find a cab outside; use it or pay the driver off. And go carefully, Jolly; we don't want more trouble with you.'

'I think I shall be able to look after myself, sir,' said Jolly. 'I will report as soon as I can.'

Rollison turned to Abbott as his servant went out.

Although the man's eyes had been open when he had first entered they were now closed, and he was feigning sleep. Rollison stepped to the bed, looking down for several seconds, and then deliberately tweaked Abbott's nose. The tweak was not painful, but it made Abbott start and wince.

'Oh, my shoulder! What—what did you do

157

that for?'

'To wake you up,' said Rollison unkindly. 'Abbott, I'm not at all sorry for you, so don't try to appeal to my sympathy. What was in that letter?'

'I've told you!' snapped Abbott. 'There were a thousand pounds, nothing else! Why haven't you sent for a doctor?'

'You've had all the doctoring you want. Why do you keep on lying?'

'I'm not!' shouted Abbott. 'And I'm badly hurt, my shoulder is terribly painful. You—you can't keep me here like this. I won't have it!'

'There are so many things you wouldn't have if the choice were yours,' said Rollison. 'It isn't and won't be. What do you know of Bennison?'

'Wh-who?'

'Don't imitate an owl, Bennison. He called on you this afternoon, and you went out to dinner with him.'

Abbott's lips twitched nervously, then he cleared his throat and muttered:

'I used to work for him; he gives me odd jobs now and again. He's a solicitor. I was a solicitor's clerk before I joined up with Gerrard. There's nothing wrong about that, is there? He's a friend of mine; he used to be a friend of Gerrard's. I don't see what it's got to do with you, anyhow.'

Abbott was soon reduced to maudlin

158

pleading. He wanted to go home, he wanted to see a doctor, he wanted the thousand pounds.

'I'll get you a doctor,' Rollison decided.

He went into the other room to telephone, and arranged for Lady Gloria and Angela to go to Braddon Place, where Angela would spend the night. He saw them off, then spoke urgently to Lane.

'Andy, telephone Scotland Yard for Superintendent Grice. Ask him to send two good men to Number Seven, to keep a special eye on Angela Gerrard. I'll be back in about half an hour.'

He went out immediately, and followed the two women. They had elected to walk, since the night was starlit, and Glory's stick could be heard tapping regularly and heavily.

They were discussing the suitability of slacks for women.

Rollison followed, but there was no threat of trouble. He watched them enter Number Seven, then strolled up and down until he saw a man approaching, walking with the near-silence created by rubber soles and heels. Rollison waited for him, just able to distinguish his face and hat, and said:

'From Superintendent Grice?'

'That's right.' The man was surprised as he peered into Rollison's face, shining a torch without making it glare into his eyes. 'Oh, Mr Rollison. Yes, sir, I'm to watch Number Seven from the front.'

159

'The back's looked after, I hope?'

'Yes, sir. I've just left the other man.'

'That's fine,' said Rollison.

He was soon sitting opposite Lane over a whisky-and-soda. By the solicitor's side was a slim volume of Maupassant's *Bel-Ami*, but Lane was giving Rollison his full attention. Rollison talked of the probability that Angela had been the intended victim, and found that Lane had already considered the possibility. He was not surprised when Lane, pursing his lips and smoothing his moustache, asked:

'Are you sure she's told you the whole truth, Rolly?'

'No. But I'll admit that I hope she has. What can you tell me of Raymond Bennison?'

Lane protested: 'I came to report on Barbicue and Gerrard, you know. I don't know more about Bennison than that he was the legal adviser to Barbicue, Gerrard & Company brokers before Gerrard's crash and Barbicue's neat skip away from the debacle. Also that Bennison was a close friend of Gerrard's.'

'What's he like?'

Lane shrugged. 'Reputable, if not particularly likeable. A clever lawyer, specializing in company-promoting and property-dealing. He does some work for Barbicue.'

'How do you know?' Rollison was intrigued.

'Some of my clients have sold property to

160

Barbicue,' said Lane. 'I'd like to meet the solicitor who hasn't a client on Barbicue's books!' He paused. 'Are you still interested in Barbicue's past? And in Gerrard's?'

'I know more of it now,' admitted Rollison, 'but I'm as receptive as ever.' He paused in his turn, but before Lane spoke again the telephone rang. 'Sorry,' said Rollison, and reached out for it. After a pause: 'Hallo, Jolly, a report so soon?'

'Yes, sir,' said Jolly unemotionally. 'I thought you should know at once that Bennison has been found dead in his own home.'

CHAPTER FIFTEEN

THE SUPREME MOMENT FOR GRICE

Andrew Lane made no protest when the Toff asked him to wait until the doctor arrived to see Abbott. He was less content with the Toff's proposal to send for a policeman to be in attendance at the flat.

'No, Rolly,' he protested. 'Keep your sense of proportion, or you'll be on the retired list. What danger can there be for me?'

'Not you,' said Rollison. 'For Freddy.'

'Abbott? Do you seriously think so?'

'He was a friend of Bennison and of Angela,'

161

said the Toff, labouring the obvious. 'Andy, I'd admit one thing to no one else in the world and shall probably wish I hadn't to you. I am scared. I gate-crashed into this affair, and I'm only just beginning to see how vicious it is. Or Barbicue's toughness. Call it resilience if you like. I hoped to get him before he found his second wind, but I've failed and I'm scared.'

'I hope I behave like you when I'm frightened,' murmured Lane. 'All right, have your policeman here. What time will you be back?'

'I wish I knew,' admitted Rollison with feeling...

'We're on Putney Hill,' Rollison's cabby said, half an hour later. 'What number did you say?'

'A house called Woodyates,' said Rollison. 'There should be several other cars outside it.'

'I see a red light,' said the cabby. 'Other side've the road, okay, sir?'

There were two cars parked on Putney Hill outside the home of Mr Bennison, and two others in the carriageway near the front door. There was no chink of light from the house itself.

One of the other 'cars' proved to be a taxi; Rollison imagined it was Jolly's, and paid off his own. Even if someone else had hired the cab he could get a lift with a police car, for he took it for granted that Grice was at 'Woodyates'. He was admitted by an oldish manservant, behind whom stood Jolly.

'Good evening, sir,' said Jolly.

'Hallo,' said Rollison. 'Is Mr Grice here?'

'Upstairs, sir, yes. I would appreciate a moment or two with you before you consult with the Superintendent,' Jolly added, and in the shadowy hall his preternaturally solemn face became positively sombre.

'Where?' asked Rollison.

'There is a small room along here, sir, which has been placed at our disposal.' Jolly led the way to a small morning room, a pleasant place of light colours and gaily-covered easy chairs, book-shelves filled with volumes all in picturesque, colourful jackets.

'What have you been doing?' asked Rollison.

'First, sir, I found this gun in Bennison's pocket. It is a .22, the size used in the attack on Barbicue.' Jolly handed it to Rollison, who said, 'Good man,' and went on: 'For the rest, I thought it would be wise to forewarn you.'

'Ah,' said Rollison, and took out a cigarette. Jolly stretched forward with a lighter, paused, and then said quietly:

'Bennison was killed in his study, stabbed in the chest several times. The instrument used was one of the small new bayonets issued to the Forces; you may find that a matter of interest. But it is not of the murder or the perpetrator that I need to talk, it is the other matter. You see, sir, a man arrived here shortly after me. On

163

a motor-cycle.'

Rollison's eyes narrowed.

'The same motor-cycle?'

'The noise it made was very much the same,' said Jolly non-committally. 'He was admitted to the house without question, and I felt that I was justified in trying to get in also. The motor-cyclist might have to report that he had failed to harm Miss Gerrard, but it occurred to me that he might have also come to commit a further crime. Consequently I rang the bell and demanded an immediate audience with Mr Bennison,' went on Jolly. 'I believe that in the same circumstances you would have taken the same course.'

'Yes,' said Rollison. 'Go on.'

'There was some difficulty and delay,' said Jolly, drawing a deep breath. 'I feel that Mr Bennison's death was in some measure my responsibility. He was dead when eventually I reached the room. It has, apparently, been his habit to allow certain visitors to leave by a side entrance, approached by a different staircase, and the motor-cyclist was obviously aware of that. He had gone when I entered. I heard the engine as I entered the room,' added Jolly. 'It was not pleasant.'

'It wouldn't be,' sympathized Rollison.

'I immediately prevailed upon the man who admitted me, sir, to telephone to Scotland Yard for Superintendent Grice, but did not think it wise to contact you. I was able to convince the man that I was virtually in authority, and was therefore able to spend some time alone in the study before the arrival of the police. There were papers on Bennison's desk, and others in his safe, which was open. I was not able to give them full attention, but I saw quite enough to tell me that Bennison was *one* of the men you want so badly.'

Rollison sat on the arm of a chair.

'I don't like your emphasis on "one".'

'I am a little puzzled by the situation myself, sir,' admitted Jolly. 'The documents are very comprehensive. They concern large consignments of foodstuffs, wines, spirits, cigarettes, cosmetics and clothes distributed in various places about the country. I was appalled! I saw enough to gather that there was a list of names and addresses of different agents disposing of the goods. A more complete and detailed record of black-market operations it would be difficult to find.'

Jolly paused, and the Toff stood up, sliding both hands into his pockets before saying very mildly:

'Very well. So Bennison is our master-mind, Jolly?'

'*A* master-mind I should imagine, sir. I have no doubt that Mr Grice will be delighted at what he has discovered upstairs, but I thought you should know in advance that the situation hardly indicts Barbicue.'

There was a tap at the door and

165

Superintendent Grice entered. Rollison saw his tired but very bright eyes, and from Grice's manner had no doubt that he felt triumphant. There was an air of repressed excitement about him, a curve at the corners of his lips which Rollison eyed without particular enthusiasm.

'The smile that wouldn't come off,' he said. 'What's happened?'

Grice smiled much more widely.

'What has Jolly been saying? If he imagined that I didn't know he was waiting down here for you, he's quite wrong. My man was watching from the landing, and reported as soon as you arrived. Rollison, I've been looking for six months—twelve months—for what I've found tonight!'

'Good,' said Rollison, heartily.

'I don't think we'll have a lot more trouble with this part of the black market,' went on Grice, with deep satisfaction. 'Nothing of any vital importance, anyhow. I don't know how it was done but you've been nicely fooled.'

'Need you look so pleased about that?'

'It doesn't worry me one way or the other,' Grice assured him. 'I don't know whether you were in any way concerned with the Bennison angle, but you will keep so much to yourself that you must expect to find bother when something is uncovered which you forgot to mention to us.' Grice chuckled, in so good a humour that Rollison felt his own depression almost worthwhile. 'Come upstairs,' added

166

Grice, 'and I'll show you some things which will make you widen your eyes.'

Rollison went up.

The police had moved the body of Bennison to a morgue, and the fingerprints and photographs had been done after Rollison's arrival. The study was a large and comfortable room lined on two walls with books and with some etchings which in normal times would have attracted Rollison's attention.

Two sergeants were sitting at either end of a large, flat-topped desk, which was covered with neat piles of paper. A chair in which Bennison had been killed was behind the desk.

Grice pushed up other chairs and then pulled a neatly kept loose-leaf book towards him.

'This is the key,' he said. 'This unlocks it all. Look at this.' He opened the loose-leaf book, and revealed a page with two rows of words. The first entries were:

Keyword	Actual
Nails	— Cigarettes
Screws	— Cigars
Varnish	— Petrol
Dust	— Tea

There was page after page with some twenty entries on each, and Rollison did no more than glance through them. Then he pushed the book aside, and Grice presented him with a series of letters, some signed by Bennison, others by men as then unknown to Rollison. They concerned consignments of nails, screws, varnish and a dozen other articles. There were letters complaining that such-and-such a shop or factory was in too dirty a condition, so that the word 'dust' was worked in quite naturally.

It was easy to understand why Grice was so pleased with himself, and Rollison admitted that Grice had every reason to be gratified. For that matter so had Rollison, except that nothing here implicated Barbicue.

Hundreds of other people were named.

Up and down the country were shopkeepers, wholesalers, and travellers, all credited with stocks of the commodities listed. There were pirate filling-stations where the 'company's' travellers obtained their petrol, another list of legal petrol suppliers who were prepared to buy on the side, at a price, knowing they could sell easily and at a good profit.

There were printers who engaged in turning out false coupons, particularly for clothes; there were sweat-shops in the East End and clothing factories in the Midlands manufacturing supplies for the black market; there were details of traffic in tyres and spare parts for cars, evidence—although it took much more than a quarter of an hour to see it all—of the fact that these parts as well as tyres, tubes, proprietary oils, anti-freeze and a dozen other things were cornered early in the war and stored against the time of acute shortage.

Rollison became absorbed.

The ramifications of the market were so wide that it was not surprising that the police had succeeded in catching only a few of the outside agents, mostly men who sold the goods to the public, rarely anyone who controlled stocks. Two large files were concerned with supplies of wines and spirits, and tobaccos and cigarettes; vast stocks of them had been accumulated and were being released gradually on to the market.

It was some time after one o'clock when Grice said:

'Now we'll have a look at the balance sheet, Rollison. He even prepared one of those!'

'A man with superb confidence,' murmured Rollison. 'I've never met him.'

'I would never have believed him capable of this,' admitted Grice.

The balance sheet was not detailed. It covered six operating months, ending the half-year June 30th, showing an analysis which was enough to make Rollison tighten his lips.

Debit				Credit			
Paid out for goods	£197,001	1	6	Receipts	£1,095,000	0	6
Paid out in commission	103,191	0	0				
Travelling and overheads	35,200	0	0				
	£335,392	1	6				
To private accounts	759,607	19	0				
	£1,095,000	0	6		£1,095,000	0	6

169

Rollison pushed the paper away, rubbed his eyes and straightened up in his chair.

'That's enough for the night, I think.'

'I haven't started,' said Grice, although his eyes were watering with overstrain. 'You see how it's divided into watertight sections, Rollison? One for spirits and wines, run by a man named Arthurson—he was inside until just before the war. Tobacco and cigarettes by Roston, squeezed out of the wholesale market before the war for selling below advertised prices; the manufacturers put him out of business. Sweets, cosmetics, perishable foods, hard foods, clothes—' Grice drew a deep breath. 'We've got them all.'

'Yes,' agreed Rollison slowly.

'The next thing I know you'll be telling me these records are faked,' said Grice.

'Oh no,' said Rollison, 'there are limits to faking, and these are beyond it. But if I were you I'd have the calls out for these gentry pretty fast, in case they skip. They might know that you've made the raid.'

'I put the calls out before you arrived, or at least while you were talking with Jolly,' Grice told him. 'Most of them will be at the Yard when I get there. It is going to take some time to get all the little men, but by noon tomorrow most of the stocks will be taken over.'

Rollison shrugged. 'I hope you're right.'

'Rolly, I didn't expect you to feel like this. I thought you were big enough not to have sour

170

grapes!' Something of the degree of his satisfaction was evinced by the fact that he used 'Rolly' instead of 'Rollison'. He leaned back in his chair, wiped his eyes on the corner of a handkerchief, and went on: 'It's exactly what we wanted; we can close the whole racket down. *Everything*. You must see that.'

'Yes,' said Rollison, and then smiled. 'Grice, I'm not trying to cry this down. If Jolly hadn't been on the spot there would have been time for the office to be emptied before Bennison was found murdered; the fact that Jolly was following the murderer almost certainly drove the man away before he could finish his job. I'll gladly bask in Jolly's credit.'

'Good,' said Grice.

'But I want Barbicue,' said Rollison.

Grice looked at him disapprovingly.

'So you aren't prepared to admit that you were wrong even now? Whoever gave you Barbicue's name knew what he was doing. He was protecting Bennison. I agree I thought differently earlier in the evening, when I thought Barbicue was going to break down. So would any man after you'd worked on him, whether he was implicated or not.'

'Oh yes,' said Rollison. 'Bill, you're wallowing in your triumph, and you can't see beyond it. Bennison must have been in this; you've got all the others, too. But what is worrying me is that you haven't caught Barbicue, and you're not likely to go after him.

171

That balance sheet shows a picking of three-quarters of a million pounds. Find the money. Bennison won't have it salted away, nor will the other men you've found here.'

Grice shrugged.

'Please yourself,' he said, and clearly only just avoided repeating 'sour grapes'. 'Bennison was a close friend of Gerrard. I wonder if this racket was beginning even then?'

'It could have been,' admitted Rollison.

'Angela Gerrard always believed that Barbicue had betrayed her father,' mused Grice. 'The betrayer could have been Bennison. That may explain why he tried to make things happier for her.'

'Did he, as much as all that?' asked Rollison.

'Well, she lived here,' said Grice. 'Didn't you know that?'

CHAPTER SIXTEEN

INTERLUDE FOR ANGELA

Rollison admitted wryly that he had not known Angela had lived here, and was compelled to listen to a homily from Grice on the wisdom of obtaining both essential and incidental information before trying to make a case. He felt that another ten minutes of Grice would be too much to bear, and left the house soon afterwards, accompanied by an equally subdued Jolly.

The driver of Jolly's cab was asleep over the wheel.

'Everyone else is happy,' said the Toff with a touch of bitterness. 'Why shouldn't we be, Jolly? Wake him up gently, and ask him if he'll mind taking us home.'

It was two o'clock when they reached the flat. There was a light in the lounge, and Lane was buried in Maupassant so deeply that he finished a paragraph before looking up and saying:

'Well, Rolly, how have you been getting on?'

'Beautifully,' said the Toff in a voice glum enough to startle Lane. 'Perfectly. I've had the night of my life. I thought I could stand being laughed at, but this has been too much.' He tossed his hat into a chair and sat opposite Lane wearily. 'Barbicue is a white-headed boy, victimized by Bennison.'

After a while he found himself talking freely and smoothly, of what had been discovered and particularly of those matters still not solved. He went on and on, and all the time there was a light in the kitchen, proving that Jolly preferred to listen than to go to bed.

Jolly had already been into the spare room to find that Abbott was sleeping heavily.

The clock chimed three, and Rollison started.

'This won't do.' He lit a cigarette. 'The last

173

one, and then we're going to bed. Out of what you've heard, Andy, can you make an intelligent guess as to who killed Bennison?'

'No,' admitted Lane, 'except that it was the motor-cyclist who attacked Angela Gerrard.'

'We think it is,' corrected Rollison. 'The evidence of a two-stroke engine can't be construed into proof. You must be as tired as I am. I—' He stopped abruptly, staring across at the older man and then going on in a low-pitched voice. 'Andy. If the same man tried to kill Angela and did kill Bennison, it could have been with the same motive. Angela and Bennison could supply vital information, dangerous information about someone unknown. In short, they knew too much.'

'Bennison didn't kill himself,' objected Lane.

'Don't you get all Grice-like. I'm thinking of the possibility that much of the stuff was planted on Bennison, who could have known that Barbicue was behind this. As Angela believed he was, Bennison might have told her.'

Lane stood up.

'You're getting too tired,' he said. 'I'm off home. If there's anything I can do in the morning, give me a ring. Do you mind if I take this with me?' he added, and when Rollison shook his head he pocketed the slim Maupassant and went to the hall for his hat and gloves.

174

'Be wise in time, Rolly. Sleep on it.'

Rollison smiled, somewhat wanly.

He was still sleeping at nine o'clock the next morning, when the rest of the occupants of the flat were awake, even Jolly, and Freddy Abbott was demanding some breakfast while giving it as his opinion that the doctor who had ordered him to stay in bed indefinitely did not know his business. He went so far as to say that he believed that the man had been coerced by Rollison.

Doubtless he would have dressed, but Jolly had removed his clothes.

At ten o'clock Jolly took in Rollison's tea. He omitted to take the papers, and when the Toff was awake enough, he asked why.

'They have not arrived yet, sir,' said Jolly, glibly.

'I don't believe you,' said Rollison flatly. 'I'm much better, Jolly; I can take it. Grice has given the Press the full story, I suppose?'

'I have no idea, sir,' insisted Jolly. 'I really have not seen them.'

With that the Toff had to be satisfied, except that he sent Jolly out for the papers while he took a bath. He felt clearer-headed, although there was an uncomfortable sense of depression within him, particularly when he contemplated the fact that Abbott was still at the flat; there was no reason for detaining the man now.

'There's a reason, all right,' Rollison argued

175

with himself, 'but I haven't found it.'

Jolly brought the papers.

There were four, and the headline in each case was in huge bold letters, describing the round-up of blackmarket suspects the previous night. Grice must have been sure of himself, or he would not have given as much information as the papers revealed. There were seven photographs beneath the headline in the *Cry*, each of the 'leaders' of different sections of the racket, Arthurson, Roston, Bennison, and others whom Grice had mentioned. Beneath the photographs were pen-pictures of the men. Grice had not given actual figures, but there were some wild guesses at the profits which served to amuse Rollison while he ate breakfast.

He finished with the papers at last, pushed them away, and then stood in front of the fireplace, smoking, and watching Jolly clear the table.

'Jolly,' he said, 'I delivered myself of a boner last night bigger than anything I've ever done before. What was it?'

'I can't say that I remember it, sir.'

'Don't lie. What was it?'

Jolly straightened up and eyed him apologetically.

'I think perhaps you are referring, sir, to a comment you made to Mr Lane. You said that you had been thinking of the possibility that much of the *data* had been planted—that was

176

the word—on Bennison, and that Bennison could have known that Barbicue was behind the affair. Angela, you said, believed that he was, and perhaps'—Jolly coughed—'Bennison confirmed that belief.'

'No!' exclaimed Rollison.

'I think you will find that is right, sir.'

'Was I as bad as that?' mourned Rollison. 'What did I mean?'

'I'm not sure that you meant anything,' said Jolly mildly. 'I think you were rather too tired to give the matter any deep thought.'

'You do, do you?' growled Rollison. 'Let me tell you, Jolly, there was skilled logic behind that comment. I thought lucidly, even if I was tongue-tied. I was trying to find a motive to cover (a) the murder of Bennison and (b) the attack on Angela Gerrard.'

'I believe that is so, sir,' conceded Jolly.

'I know it's so! Listen, Jolly. Assume that Barbicue sent the assailant. Indulge me that far. And wait. Why should he want Bennison dead? Because he wanted Bennison found with all the evidence. Why should he want Angela dead? Because Angela lived at Bennison's house, and Bennison *might* have told her something of his suspicions. Remember she was already brimful of malice for Barbicue? She would be easily persuaded.'

'I see what you mean, sir.' Jolly was a little more impressed.

'That's what I meant last night,' went on
177

Rollison with feeling. 'Now think back. There is another reason for Bennison's murder. Barbicue knew that, or was afraid that, the racket was on its last legs. Some men would have followed it and finished and died with it. Not Barbicue. It paid well, it netted him something like a million pounds. With that million, he financed his legal business, his buying and selling. He is a rich man, and need not continue to make money out of the market. So what does he do? He closes the market, presents the police with a perfect victim, duly dead and therefore silent, and laughs at me. That is reasonable, isn't it?'

'It sounds eminently reasonable, sir,' admitted Jolly. 'The difficulty is—'

'Go on, what is it?'

'Finding the necessary evidence.'

'Even I'd seen that. It shouldn't be so difficult.'

'No, sir?'

'No. The motor-cyclist with a bent for murder. He would know who gave him his orders.'

'So all we have to do is to find the murderer, sir; yes,' said Jolly mildly.

'Oh, go and wash up,' said Rollison irritably. 'That was sarcasm of the *n*th degree. "*All* we have to do is find the murderer". Let me tell you, Jolly, that you saw him and you saw him twice. What was he like?'

'He was huddled up in a big coat, and his

178

collar was turned up,' said Jolly. 'He wore goggles, and I'm afraid it would be quite impossible for me to identify him. I have given the police all possible particulars of the motor-cycle. They might be able to trace him through that, although the number, AJX4, was doubtless a false one. It was a Douglas two-stroke, painted green, and with a red cushion on the pillion.'

'Painted green, with a red cushion on the pillion,' echoed Rollison slowly. As slowly, he went on: 'Jolly, leave everything and go down to see Lizzie Diver. Tell her you're looking for such a motor-cycle. Then go to the other pubs and places, get all the boys you can looking for that machine. They'll tell you or me if they know about it, whereas they won't tell the police. Look out Joe Batty—you remember Joe?'

'The man who warned you that James Lett had been inquiring about you? Yes, sir.'

'Ask Joe to spread the news around that we want that motor-cycle. Get the East End turned upside down for it. You want word of James Lett, too; he'll be known well enough. Get it for me, they'll be garrulous enough. Unless I miss my guess there'll be a lot of jubilation in the East End today, Jolly. They're free of the market, there'll be no more threatening touts, no more beatings-up. Grice will be busy dealing with everything that could be connected with it. It'll be a holiday such as they haven't had for years. Go to it, Jolly; we want that murderer.'

'Very good,' said Jolly soberly, and went for his bowler hat and rolled umbrella. Holding one in each hand, he presented himself again, and said: 'What about Abbott, sir?'

'I'll look after him,' promised the Toff.

He went into the kitchen, and from a drawer took a small magnifying glass, from another a block of wood with a steel plate on one side. He took the gun Jolly had obtained from Bennison, and fired a single shot into the wood. That done, he dug the bullet from the wood— the steel had prevented a complete piercing— and examined it, with that from Barbicue's room, under the glass. 'One and the same,' he commented quietly. 'So Bennison was after Barbicue.'

It was some twenty minutes after Jolly had gone that the front-door bell rang. Rollison opened it, and was not really surprised to see Angela, nor even the expression on her face. He was reminded of the moment when he had seen her entering the 'Splendide's' lift, with Barbicue in pursuit. She carried several newspapers under her arm, and entered tight-lipped.

'Well, Angela,' began the Toff. 'Did you have—'

'Do you know anything about *that*?' interrupted Angela sharply.

Rollison wished it could be otherwise, but
180

knew that there must be an interlude for Angela. He was not happy, for he had gathered how fond she had been of Bennison.

He said: 'Too much evidence was there, Angela.'

'So you did it,' she said in the same tense voice. 'That's why you sent Jolly to ask me for his address.' She drew a deep breath. 'If I'd known, you would never have had it! I would have seen you dead first!'

'Angela,' said Rollison quietly, 'you're as wrong now as you were wrong with Freddy yesterday. If Jolly had left there five minutes earlier, Bennison would not have been dead.'

'No?' She sneered the word. 'And this wouldn't have been published, I suppose?'

'You've the wrong end of the stick,' said Rollison, still quietly. 'The police discovered all that, I didn't. It was all there in Bennison's study, each piece of evidence quite conclusive. I didn't like it. I didn't want it. I wanted Barbicue.'

'And now he's laughing at you, at me, at Bennison!' cried Angela. 'If Barbicue had died this wouldn't have happened. He's done it all. *You* saved Barbicue; you told me you did!'

'If you're going to talk in italics we can't do anything about it,' protested Rollison. 'We have one thing in common, however. We want Barbicue. I think we shall get him before we're through. But I don't think we shall be able to

181

do anything to save Bennison's reputation. I'm afraid Bennison was deeply involved. He and Barbicue worked together. Sometimes I think they also worked against one another in competition, probably deceiving one another as often as they could.'

'It can't be true. Bennison wouldn't—'

'I think that much of the evidence was planted on Bennison,' said Rollison insistently, 'but not all of it.' He put his hand to his pocket and drew out Bennison's automatic, showing it to her. 'Have you ever seen this before?'

She was startled. 'I don't know,' she amended in some confusion. 'I—I've seen one like it.'

'At Bennison's house?'

'What does that matter?' demanded Angela. 'What are you trying to do now?'

'This was in Bennison's room,' said Rollison. 'I managed to get it without showing it to the police. I've fired a shot from it, and compared the markings on the bullet with those on one which nearly killed Barbicue. Do you know anything about ballistics?'

'Bal-ballistics? What do you mean?'

'Then you don't know. The science of projectiles, particularly of bullets. Under a microscope it is possible to find whether a certain bullet was fired from a certain gun. This gun fired the bullets which nearly killed Barbicue. Bennison fired those shots, Angela, and Barbicue knew that. One or the other had to die; it was the old, old story of a quarrel among thieves. You knew who fired it, didn't you? That's why you were frightened that Barbicue would catch you; you were afraid he would make you talk.'

He finished, watching her closely.

He felt sure that it was true, and believed that she had tried hard to protect Bennison, despite deep suspicions of him. How much more did she know?

As she did not speak, he said:

'Isn't that all true? It needn't come out, you know, even if it is. In any case it won't worry Bennison now.'

She drew a short, sharp breath.

'Oh, dear God! I—'

Then the door of the spare room opened and Abbott stepped through, clad in a pair of Rollison's pyjamas. They were much too long for him and although he had turned them up at the legs and sleeves he could not hide that, nor the fact that they were too tight across his chest and his buttocks.

'Of course it's true!' he snapped. 'She knew it all the time. Bennison always hated Barbicue. I can tell you something else, now that it's come out: the only reason I kept quiet was because Bennison had been a good friend—'

Angela spun round towards him.

'You hold your tongue! The only reason you kept quiet was because you made money on

183

the side!'

'I'll say what I like!' declared Abbott, striking an attitude which did not become him in red and blue stripes. 'After the way you've behaved, *you've* no right to my sympathy. I'm loyal to my friends, and I was loyal to Bennison but I knew he was going to try to kill Barbicue. Why, I saw him go into your room that morning! You must have known, too. You knew what was in my envelope; you pretended you didn't, but you must have done. What about that?'

Angela tightened her lips and glared at him.

'So there was something besides a thousand pounds,' said Rollison quietly.

'Supposing there was?' Abbott's voice rose up to a screech. 'Listen to me, Rollison! Bennison was going to frame Barbicue; he told me he had plenty of evidence. He wrote it out, and gave it to me. I—'

He stopped abruptly.

'Go on,' murmured the Toff. 'Go on, Abbott, I want to know all about your nasty little mind, and the way it works. What did you do with it?'

Abbott licked his lips. Even he could not maintain a steady gaze at either Rollison or Angela, but began to speak clearly enough for them both to hear.

'I wanted money badly, you know that, and a thousand wasn't enough. I took the report to Barbicue, and offered it to him. He laughed

184

when he'd read it, and said he could answer all the charges. I—I didn't know whether it was true or not. I had to bring the report away. It's a wonder he bought my house from me, then, knowing I worked with Bennison.'

Angela clenched her fists.

Rollison said scathingly: 'You didn't know whether it was true? You nasty little tyke, you knew what Barbicue would do to get those papers, you handed your notecase to Angela so that no one would attack you, and I'll bet you let him know that Angela had them. It's why he wanted to see Angela so badly that morning.' His voice grew a little less searing. He was thinking fast as he talked, and there was even a note of satisfaction in his words. 'He sent David and the man in brown after it, and because David knew too much he had him killed. He had the indictment from Bennison, and knew that he had to work quickly then, so he planted the papers on Bennison, and killed him. So he's sitting pretty. He's afraid only that Angela might have been in Bennison's confidence, and fears that she has talked to me. The danger for Barbicue is from you and me, Angela, and no one else.'

'What—what about me?' exclaimed Abbott. 'I could give him away. I'm in as much danger as you are; that's why I've stayed here.' He was shivering, as if putting the knowledge of danger into words had scared him. 'What are you going to do about it? Barbicue won't lose

185

time, you ought to know that. What are you going to do?'

CHAPTER SEVENTEEN

EVERYTHING BUT BARBICUE?

Rollison put both hands deep in his pockets, eyeing Abbott without speaking. The man appeared so frightened of Barbicue's vengeance that he could not keep from shivering. In Angela's eyes as she regarded the man to whom she had been engaged there was a scathing contempt.

'Can't we pack him in a parcel, and send him to Barbicue?' asked Angela tensely.

'You little cat!'

'We can't do it, although it's a bright idea.' Rollison paused, and then added as if to himself: 'We have everything but Barbicue.'

'He might send for us any minute!' screeched Abbott.

'We could go to him,' mused Rollison; 'but before we do that we want the man in brown, the gunman who held us up at Braddon Place. Your evidence isn't enough; it would look as if I'd inspired it. Had either of you seen the man in brown before?'

Abbott said 'no', and Angela shook her head.

186

'We need to pray that we'll get him,' said Rollison. 'Now—do either of you know about a rendezvous at or near Epping?'

'Epping!' exclaimed Abbott. 'W-why, what do you know about it?'

'Not enough. What do you?'

Abbott drew a deep breath, and then turned away.

'N-nothing, nothing at all, I thought—'

Rollison reached him in two strides, and gripped his wrist. For a moment he thought that the man would put up a fight, but there was no courage in Abbott.

'Mind my shoulder, you're hurting! I—I had to go to Epping sometimes to get—get some stores for Bennison.'

'Just where?'

'To—to Bennison's other house.'

'What kind of stores?'

'A few—a few bottles of brandy, and that kind of thing; he didn't keep much in London; most of it was in the country. He only kept that store for a few of the better clients; he had a little of everything there. It had been there for a long time, before he bought the house from—'

Abbott paused.

He was staring at Angela, and Angela was looking at him with her eyes so bright with anger that Rollison imagined she was having to force herself not to strike him.

'Go on,' she said with dangerous quiet. 'Go on, say it. Before he bought it from my father.'

'Well, he did, didn't he?'

'What *is* this?' demanded the Toff.

Angela said: 'It's easy enough, Rolly.' She drooped suddenly, as if feeling very weary. 'Bennison bought it from Father just before the crash. We'd always lived there, but Father tried to keep things going, and sold it. Bennison gave him a good price, but rented it to us for next to nothing. It was useless when Father died. I've never wanted to go there since he killed himself in the study.' She was very pale. 'Now Freddy's suggesting that Father knew about the market. He's—' She looked at Abbott dully, and then threw up her hands. 'I can't find words.'

'I can understand that,' said Rollison. 'I need to get to this place quickly. Just where is it?'

'It's on the edge of the forest, a house called "Greystones",' said Angela. 'It's really in Loughton, not Epping. You can't miss it if you're on the main London Road. But you won't get Barbicue there,' she said. 'I thought you were after Barbicue.'

'His men have been in the area,' Rollison said.

'I don't see that it means anything.'

She broke off as the telephone rang.

Rollison hoped it would be Jolly, but instead heard Grice's voice, still full of satisfaction.

'Good morning, Rolly. How are you?'

'Still sour,' said Rollison, keeping an eye on

188

Abbott and Angela.

Grice chuckled.

'Aren't you over it yet? I've some more news, too. We've found most of the warehouses where the stores are kept, enough almost to make an increase in some of the coupon values, I think! You ought to know that the last arrest reported made the hundredth.'

'Nice work,' approved Rollison warmly. 'As I've already said, everyone and everything but Barbicue.'

'Are you still chasing that hare? Oh—there's another thing I thought you would like to know,' went on Grice. 'Bennison has another house, in Loughton, a place called "Greystones". It's just inside the forest. We've picked up James Lett, and he's told us that he often saw Bennison there. And'—Grice grew a little more sober-voiced—'I don't like having to give you your *conge,* Rollison, but Lett has told me how you forced the information out of him. He worked for Bennison, of course, and Bennison gave him instructions to name Barbicue if ever he had to name anyone.'

Rollison's fingers tightened on the receiver.

For a moment he could not think. Certainly he had never been forced to swallow quite so bitter a pill. He steadied himself, and made some comment which could not have been too outrageous, for Grice said:

'Yes, it makes it comprehensive. How comprehensive we don't quite know. I think

189

we'll need a month to find all the ramifications. Meanwhile, is there anything else *you* want to know?'

'Yes. Are you watching Barbicue?' asked Rollison.

'Now, Rolly,' protested Grice. 'We haven't time to waste.'

'You are positively convinced that he's not involved?'

'Of course I am,' said Grice. 'I was reasonably sure once we found Bennison, but Lett's evidence is quite conclusive.'

'Tell me,' said Rollison slowly, 'who killed Bennison, and why?'

'The "who" isn't known yet,' said Grice, 'but the "why" is. Lett has made a complete confession and a full statement, and it includes further unpleasant facts about Bennison, who also tricked and cheated the man who worked for him. He had told Lett that he was afraid for his life, that two or three of the men he had used but afterwards allowed to be sentenced, were looking for him. He bought their silence by promising them a lump sum when they came out of prison, and then refused the pay-out. The men knew that their evidence was useless to you—or thought it was—and carried out their own private vengeance. One of them killed him.'

'Balderdash.'

'If you will take it like that, there's nothing more I can say,' said Grice, huffily.

190

He rang off, leaving Rollison staring at the instrument. A movement from Angela stirred him at last, and he turned to regard her.

'What has happened?' she asked.

'The police have found "Greystones", so that's off,' said Rollison. 'They're also quite happy about Barbicue, but he's not off.'

'Can't you tell the police what I've told you?' demanded Abbott wildly.

'And very convincing that would be,' said the Toff bleakly. 'I've told you, it would look as if I had put you up to the story. If you had that report we might be able to do something, but any posthumous statement from Bennison would get little attention; Barbicue's found an answer to everything. Everything normal,' he added slowly. 'If there's a chance, Jolly will find it with the motor-cycle.'

'What motor-cycle?' asked Abbott.

'Forget it,' said Rollison. 'Do you know where your clothes are?'

'No, that confounded man of yours hid them.'

'They're somewhere in the flat,' said Rollison, and then stopped abruptly, for there was a noise in the kitchen. A moment later he laughed at temporary fears, for Jolly had returned by the back door.

Jolly regarded Angela and the pyjama-clad Abbott without a change of expression; and said:

'I have initiated inquiries, sir, and if

191

anything is discovered it will be reported here.'

'Good,' said Rollison. 'Give Abbott his clothes, and if necessary help him on with them. I'm going out.'

'May I inquire where you're going, sir?'

'To look for the motor-cycle,' said Rollison. 'I might see it passing by. Coming, Angela?'

'I suppose I might as well,' said Angela.

If she was surprised at the eagerness in Rollison's manner when he reached the street, she said nothing. She held her head high, but was tight-lipped; it was easy to imagine that she was looking into a past which had been full of shadows.

At the end of Gresham Terrace there was a telephone kiosk; Rollison stopped by it and said:

'I'm going in here a moment. Will you wait?'

'Why on earth didn't you phone from the flat?'

'I forgot,' said Rollison mendaciously.

Angela stood by, and he was able to watch the road in both directions after he had put his coins in and dialled his own number.

'Mr Rollison's residence,' said Jolly a moment later.

'Jolly.' Rollison kept his voice low, and yet sounded urgent. 'Let Abbott go, and follow him.'

'Of course, sir,' said Jolly. 'You had not countermanded the previous instructions. I will see to it.'

192

Rollison smiled, and 'Good man,' turned his smile towards Angela and then stepped out of the kiosk.

The sharp note of a motor-cycle engine impinged itself on his ears as the door closed. Angela appeared to notice nothing, but Rollison gripped her arm and backed against the wall, where the kiosk offered some cover. The staccato two-stroke drew nearer; the motor-cycle turned the corner.

Its rider was huddled in a big coat, and wore goggles. The machine was brown, not green, but on the pillion was a red cushion.

'What—' began Angela.

'Hush!' urged Rollison.

The motor-cycle passed them. As he went Rollison imagined him making an attack with a gun or a knife, and felt a peculiar sense of anti-climax when nothing happened and the motor-cyclist went along the Terrace, cutting out his engine as he passed 55G. He slowed down and straddled along with his feet touching the ground from time to time, and Rollison thought that he was going to make a call on the flat.

Apparently the man changed his mind, for he went on to the end of the street, then turned back.

'The motor-cyclist!' exclaimed Angela.

'Not really,' scoffed Rollison. 'Sometimes you do yourself less than justice, at others you're nearly brilliant. Is he just here to keep an eye on us, do you think?'

'What can I think?'

'There's something in that question,' admitted Rollison. 'I wonder how long it will take Freddy to get dressed?'

'What *are* you talking about? Why are we staying here?'

'I have had what you call an idea, Angela dear, and it's been with me for twenty-four hours, although I haven't had the wit to see it.'

Fifteen minutes later he glanced at his wrist-watch.

'They shouldn't be long now, and we've been seen by fifty people. I think they've probably come to the conclusion that you're not talking to me with any moral purpose in mind.' He smiled one-sidedly as he looked along the Terrace, and then added sharply:

'Freddy's coming.'

He put his hand to his holster and drew his gun as Frederick Abbott stepped into the Terrace from 55G.

The motor-cyclist also drew a hand from his pocket, and Angela would have cried out at the sight of the gun had Rollison not put a hand to her lips.

CHAPTER EIGHTEEN

'WHY PICK ON ME?' ASKS BARBICUE

Rollison did not squeeze his trigger at once. The motor-cyclist did.

Both Rollison and Angela saw the flame from his gun but heard little more than a sneezing sound which would certainly not attract attention elsewhere. The bark of the two-stroke was much louder as the motor-cyclist pressed his foot down, and then fired again, both times towards Abbott.

Both bullets missed.

Abbott swung round a shade before the first, as if warned intuitively of danger, and flung himself down at the second. Angela pulled herself free and began to run along the Terrace. The motor-cyclist was roaring towards the end of the street. Rollison drew a deep breath and fired, saying:

'Angela, you little fool. Angela!'

His bullet struck the motor-cycle, not the cyclist.

It was enough to send the machine careering across the road out of control. A shot doubtless intended for Angela smashed a window with a loud report. Machine and cyclist crashed, while from the door of 55G Jolly came running, heedless of the possibility of another shot from the cyclist.

With the Toff running in one direction and preparing to shoot again, people hurrying from doorways and shouting from windows, the motor-cyclist easing himself from his machine and levelling his automatic, Jolly paused halfway across the road. For a split second he stood quite still; then he threw his umbrella javelin-fashion at the motor-cyclist, judging the moment to a nicety. The ferrule caught the man in the face, making the next shot go wide. Jolly crossed the intervening space in the canter, and deliberately kicked the automatic away.

'Nice going, Jolly,' said Rollison, and pulled up alongside.

Angela was helping Freddy to his feet. Freddy looked dazed, and limped to a granite gate-post. A dozen people asked shrill, urgent questions, and two policemen came hurrying from different corners.

Rollison saw all that, and called:

'Angela, come here a minute.'

She obeyed; the expression in his face was enough to make her. It was one which made her forget everything else—as if Rollison was seeing the dawn of a new and glorious day yet realizing the possibility of disaster.

Abbott continued to lean against the post; the rest of the crowd were crowding about Rollison, Angela, Jolly and the injured man, including the police.

196

Then into the Terrace came a luxurious limousine, purring its way along and hugging the near-side kerb. Even then it forced members of the crowd to surge away, although indubitably it slowed down.

A man who lost his footing clutched at Rollison, who was staring at the car as it passed between him and Abbott, leaving Abbott isolated on the opposite pavement. Rollison could not see the man in the tonneau of the big car, although he saw the chauffeur clearly.

'Sorry!' the man gasped, but continued to clutch, so that Rollison had to turn.

As the car passed there was another muffled sound as of a shot. Rollison heard it but was too late to prevent the damage.

A bullet struck the motor-cyclist in the head; a dozen people screamed. Angela drew a deep breath, while Rollison growled at the man who had impeded him.

An automatic fell in the roadway, near the car.

The car travelled on, and turned a corner. It was impossible to stop it, although Rollison shook the man off and levelled his gun as Abbott came running from 55G. He passed between the Toff and the car, and prevented a shot.

'Barbicue!' screamed Abbott. 'He was in that car, I saw him; he—Good God!' The car disappeared while Abbott stared at the motor-cyclist. 'He's—he's shot!'

'He's dead and can't talk for or against
Barbicue. But Barbicue wouldn't be fool
enough to come into the open like that,'
Rollison said harshly.

'It was him, I tell you! It was!'

A policeman was already hurrying towards
the telephone kiosk.

'*Now* I mean to know what's been
happening,' declared another policeman. 'I
want your gun, sir, too.' He held a hand
towards Rollison.

'Later, constable. Jolly, give him as full a
statement as you can.'

He turned, pushed the constable to one side,
and went hurrying along the street, picking up
the automatic in the road as he went. Shouts
followed him, and two or three people tried to
stop him, but he shouldered them aside.
Somehow Angela contrived to get away from
the crowd, and he heard her running after him.
Abbott was still raising his voice and shouting,
while Rollison saw a taxi passing the end of the
Terrace. He called and sprinted.

The driver stopped.

Rollison waited just long enough for Angela
to join him, bundled her into the cab, and said:

'The Splendide Hotel, cabby.'

Angela was gasping for breath.

'Where—are—we—going?' A long pause.
'Was—it—Barbi—'

'Freddy said so,' said Rollison brusquely.
'Save your breath, Angela; you'll probably

198

need it. We're going to see Barbicue, if Barbicue is in the "Splendide".' He opened the glass partition between him and the driver, and said more loudly: 'When you've dropped us, go on to the nearest telephone box and call Superintendent Grice at the Yard. Tell him that Rollison advises him to get to the "Splendide" without losing a minute. Give him an outline of what you saw.'

'Okay, sir.'

There were crowds about the streets leading to the 'Splendide', and a stream of people were entering and leaving the mammoth establishment. The familiar face of the commissionaire loomed in the window as the cab drew up, a man who nodded as he said:

''Morning, sir.'

'Is Mr Barbicue in?' demanded Rollison.

'Yes, sir. He went up from breakfast 'arf an hour ago,' said the commissionaire, who on the previous day had been opening and shutting the door of the lounge. That morning, perhaps because it was much cooler, the lounge doors were allowed to remain open, and he was on other door duties.

'He's here!' exclaimed Angela. 'Rolly, he couldn't have been in that car!'

'Apparently not,' said Rollison.

He paid the cabby his due and the commissionaire stared at the note, then hustled Angela into the foyer, where the usual crowd was gathered and the usual urgent requests

199

were hurtled towards the unruffled queens of the reception desk. A lift had just descended, and Rollison stepped in behind Angela. Two others joined them, a man and a woman.

'Fifth, please,' said Rollison.

'Seventh,' said the other man.

They stepped into the fifth floor hallway and then went hurrying along the passages, where they had first met. Rollison turned right and then left, remembering the directions to Barbicue's office-cum-bedroom clearly and without troubling to read the indicators.

The door of Room 547 was closed.

'I don't believe that man downstairs,' Angela said. 'Barbicue will be gone; he can't be here.'

'We'll know in a moment,' Rollison pointed out, and tapped on Barbicue's door.

There was a pause, a footstep, and then the door opened.

Barbicue stood facing them.

Angela exclaimed, and gripped Rollison's arm. Barbicue stepped back a pace, his surprise fading and a smile replacing it. He even stretched out his right hand, but withdrew it with dignity when he saw that Rollison was not going to respond.

'My dear Major, I'm delighted to see you! And Miss Gerrard—I could hardly ask for more. Come in, come in!'

'We're coming,' said Rollison grimly.

Barbicue ignored his manner, and

200

apologized for having no clerk; he had not yet had the heart to try to replace David, he declared unctuously. He led the way into the inner room, and pushed armchairs towards his visitors.

'I will stand up,' he declared, 'it will serve the purpose of a constitutional, eh, Major?'

'How long have you been here?' demanded Angela.

Barbicue turned puzzled eyes towards her.

'Since about midnight last night, my dear. I was working late and have only just returned from breakfast.' He proffered cigarettes. 'Rollison, I won't pretend that I am not delighted to see you, and immensely relieved. I was afraid that in view of your attitude last night even the developments of which you have doubtless read in the Press would not convince you of your mistake. But I am relieved beyond all measure at your visit. After all, you are a logical man, a reasonable man. You perhaps know that Bennison tried to implicate me?' He gazed wide-eyed and outraged at the Toff, who had not taken a chair but was standing by the side of one. 'Have you heard?'

'How did you hear?' demanded Rollison.

'I had a young man here from the *Daily Echo* not an hour ago,' said Barbicue. 'For once I broke my hitherto unalterable rule of seeing no one before breakfast! This reporter told me that there was a report that Bennison, through a man named—now what was his name?—

Lett, that's right, Lett—had at one time made a statement which incriminated me.' He stared into Rollison's bleak eyes, and his smile grew a little strained. Yet he made a fine show of confidence, exclaiming: 'Lett! Of course you mentioned the name to me, that is how you first conceived your suspicions of me!' He laughed; the laughter had a hollow note. 'No wonder you were so sure of yourself, my dear Major!'

'I am sure,' said Rollison.

'You—you *persist*!' exclaimed Barbicue, and his smile disappeared. 'Rollison, this is too much.'

'Are we getting anywhere?' exclaimed Angela.

'I fear not,' said Barbicue, now cold and distant. 'I welcomed this visit, but now—'

'Barbicue,' interrupted the Toff, 'I told you when I first saw you that our meeting was a sentence of death, and so it's proved. Even though you had Bennison murdered, as well as David, who might have talked; even though you made the Letts believe their leader was Bennison, or thought you succeeded in that. You see, Barbicue, the man on the motor-cycle has been caught.'

Barbicue stared, blank-faced.

'I do not understand you.'

'The man in brown, who was with David,' continued Rollison. 'The man who tried to kill Angela last night, and did kill Bennison. The man who came again today to try to lay

202

another false trail. You've had to work too fast, Barbicue; there are gaps in your story and they can't be filled in.'

'Nonsense!' cried Barbicue. 'Utter nonsense!'

He had lost much of his colour, and Rollison felt more sure than ever of his guilt, but still could not see exactly how to break him. Barbicue thrust a hand into his pocket, then stepped to the wall, near a bell-push.

'I shall ring for assistance, Rollison. When the maid comes I shall tell her to ask the porter to come and see you out. I have had enough.'

'Don't call for help yet, Barbicue, wait until you really need it,' Rollison said. 'I've told you I know how you worked. I know you planted the papers on Bennison, the final documents which made him seem to be in this thing much further than his neck. You had to have a foot in both camps, didn't you? You had to have a man who would watch Bennison for you, and someone who had access to his house.'

Barbicue was standing and staring at him.

Angela sat eyeing Rollison, her eyes very bright.

'There was such a man,' went on the Toff. 'More than one, perhaps, but one for certain. By name Abbott—Freddy Abbott. Now that he knows he's trapped, he will talk. Don't you think so, Barbicue?'

CHAPTER NINETEEN

THREATS ARE WORTH WHILE

Barbicue's face was set rigidly as he looked at the Toff. Between the two men the silence was unbroken for fully twenty seconds; it might have lasted longer had Angela not said in a flat voice:

'Rolly, you're absurd! Freddy just tried to—to persuade us it was Barbicue.'

'He didn't mean it,' the Toff assured her. 'He had seen the man in the tonneau and knew that it wasn't Barbicue; his outburst sounded wild but it was sane enough. Freddy wouldn't betray Barbicue; they work too closely together.'

'You have taken complete leave of your senses,' declared Barbicue harshly.

'Leave the cliches, and drop the grand manner,' said Rollison. 'Now that I've got Abbott, I've got you. He tried very hard to keep himself in the clear, and even tried to help you again by killing the motor-cyclist. That left only the pair of you who knew the truth. I was very late in thinking of him,' he admitted, 'but a cog slipped into place. When you sent David and the motor-cyclist to get that envelope at Haddon Place, I could have stopped their escape but for Abbott, who cannoned into me.'

204

Barbicue lowered himself into a chair.

'Go on,' he said with masterly patience and a gesture of sublime resignation. 'Until you have worked the nonsense out of your system I shall not hear the end of it. Go on, Major Rollison, but be as quick as you can.'

'It won't take long,' said the Toff. 'Abbott stopped me then, and when I realized that was deliberate and not accidental, the rest followed quite naturally. He went away, and saw Bennison. He took Bennison out to an early supper while the documents and records were planted in "Woodyates". Meanwhile you had been watching me, through the motor-cyclist—what's his name, by the way?'

'Your cheap tricks do not amuse me,' sneered Barbicue.

'Too bad. We'll call him Green; it was the colour of his motor-bike until he had it repainted after the police call sent out for him. You knew that Angela and the others were at the "Regal" because he telephoned you. He knew that I was here. So you arranged for him to attack Angela—'

'My dear sir! Why, pray, should I wish to do that?'

'Didn't I tell you? Bennison was very suspicious that you were going to frame him. He might have talked to Angela, but he didn't; he was more loyal than you in every way. Abbott was waiting at the flat, another ruse to indicate his own complete innocence, and to

205

keep suspicion away. Thanks to Jolly, Abbott received what was intended for Angela, but as it appeared to put him in the clear he didn't complain very much. He even agreed to stay at the flat because he thought he could find out how much I really knew. Anything he heard last night helped precious little; I was much too woolly-headed. He could have got away, of course, but preferred to stay there. It was such a perfect alibi for him.'

'You appear to think that a matter for admiring reflection,' said Barbicue heavily. 'I do not believe you have any evidence at all against Abbott.'

Rollison smiled at him brightly.

'I've got Abbott as tightly as I have you. I won't list the other factors pointing to Abbott until we get to something you can't know. He was shot at by Green—remember Green, who owned a motor-cycle?—who had a sitting bird shot but missed too easily. Abbott turned round in alarm at the first shot—*before it came!* I saw him move before I saw the flash and that told me what I wanted. It was a faked attack on Abbott, intended to free him of all possible suspicion. You had to make sure of that, Barbicue, so you had Green waiting to take the pot-shot. Abbott could have betrayed you. Your only insurance was to see him safe. Not dead, for although the police would think the murderer of Bennison a man with a known grudge, Abbott's death would have raised new

206

questions. However, I got Green alive. Abbott realized then that if Green were taken prisoner he might talk, because at least one attempted murder could be pinned securely to him. Abbott hurried back towards my flat, desperate until a car came along. It was just an innocent car with an innocent driver. Abbott fired from the porch, killing Green and yelling blue murder that you were in the car, knowing full well that you weren't. It looked as if he wanted you caught. Actually he wanted to convince me that he was no friend of yours.'

The Toff paused, and leaned back against the wall.

'That's the story of Abbott, Barbicue, and the story that is going to write *finis* for you.'

Barbicue regarded him icily.

'Is that *all*, Major Rollison?'

'Hook, line and sinker.'

'Good day to you,' said Barbicue. 'Miss Gerrard, I advise you to be more careful in selecting your friends. If you spend much time with Major Rollison, you will find yourself in an unenviable position.'

'Yes, of course,' said Rollison, and took his hand to his pocket. He held an automatic—the automatic he had picked up in Gresham Terrace.

Barbicue started and stared at it.

'Put that away, at once!'

'You've never liked lethal weapons, have you?' mused the Toff. 'But I'm not going to take a chance on letting you go. There will never be a stronger case against you. Yet I don't propose to let you live.'

Angela drew a sharp breath.

Barbicue backed a pace.

'Rollison, don't be a fool! That would be murder.'

'Oh I don't know,' said Rollison, but although he spoke casually there was a cold glint in his eyes. He held the gun lightly, took out a handkerchief and wiped the handle carefully, then held it, with the handkerchief, pointing towards Barbicue. The man backed away, while Angela said:

'Rolly, be careful!'

'I am being very careful,' said Rollison. 'I'm making sure that Barbicue pays for all he's done, that he feels some of the pain and terror he has inflicted on hundreds of little tradesmen like Sammy Diver, that he pays for Bennison's murder. More—that he pays for cheating the country, for the sabotage known as the black-market. This war effort wants everything we can give it, and he's made a filthy profit out of it. A foul profit, out of food and clothes that the people need. He's robbed fools, he's forced some commodities into short supply, but far worse than anything else he has helped to divert material and labour away from the war effort, and made money out of the deaths of tens of thousands. This war is everyone's war, and anyone cheating in it is cheating everyone.

You're a ghoul, Barbicue.'

He paused and eyed Angela.

'You want to see him dead, don't you? You hate him for what he did to your father and to Bennison, don't you? You'll swear that he was shot in a struggle, won't you?'

Angela gasped:

'Oh, dear God! Rolly, you mustn't do it! That's what the law's for; you mustn't do it!'

'*You* feel like that? About Barbicue?' Rollison stared at her, apparently aghast. The gun pointed towards the floor for long enough to allow Barbicue to take a step towards him.

He snatched the automatic, leaving the handkerchief in Rollison's hand.

'Rolly!' exclaimed Angela. 'Rolly, be careful!'

Barbicue backed away swiftly, the gun pointing towards Rollison. His eyes were narrowed, his lips parted to show his fine teeth.

'Don't move!' he snapped. 'Don't move, Rollison!'

The Toff looked at him, leaned back against the wall, and smiled. Not only did he smile, he made it look benign.

'I won't move, Barbicue,' he said gently. 'You took that nicely, didn't you? That gun, Barbicue. It's the one which killed Green. Remember Green? It's got your fingerprints on it now. You wouldn't mind helping in a little lie like that, Angela, would you?'

209

CHAPTER TWENTY

'A WELL-DESERVED REST,' SAYS JOLLY

The room was very silent.

Angela stared at the Toff, who was standing by a cabinet, his hand on the London directories, and the Toff towards Angela. Barbicue tightened his grip on the automatic, but his face was turning grey.

'Would you?' insisted Rollison at last. 'You know that he's behind it, Angela, as well as I do. All you have to do is to agree with me when I say that Barbicue took the gun from his pocket to threaten us. He'll hang, then, for the murder of Green.'

Angela said very slowly:

'Yes. I—I saw him take it out.'

'Why, you—' screamed Barbicue, and raised the gun.

It was quivering in his grip; his lips were shaking, there was a green tinge to his pallor. He fired once, but the bullet went at least a foot wide, for Rollison swept the directories from the top of the cabinet towards him and spoiled his aim.

Rollison reached him, gripped his wrist, twisted until he screamed again, and the gun dropped from his fingers to the carpet.

'Don't touch it!' Rollison warned Angela. 'We want his prints.'

'It's a lie, it's a lie, it's a lie!' screamed Barbicue. 'I didn't shoot anyone. I—Rollison! Rollison!' He gasped the name, stopped trying to release himself, gripped the lapels of Rollison's tunic and went on: 'Rollison, tell the truth, tell the truth! You wouldn't see me hanged for something I didn't do.'

'I'd even attend the ceremony,' said Rollison. 'We came straight here. You were up in this room when the man was killed. You've no alibi, for you were working here alone. It's easy to slip out of a hotel like this and return without being seen.'

Barbicue drew a sobbing breath.

'No, no! Angela!' He turned from Rollison and stumbled towards the girl. 'Angela, you wouldn't lie! You wouldn't lie about that! I would be hanged.'

'You should have been hanged a year ago,' said Angela coldly.

'No!' Barbicue put his hands to her shoulders, shook her. 'No, you wouldn't allow it, not Gerrard's daughter, you wouldn't allow it!' He looked into her face and saw it unrelenting, and stepped back. 'They won't believe it!' he gasped. 'I'll tell them you lied! I'll tell them just what you did!'

Rollison said: 'Fingerprints don't lie.'

There was a near-silence again, broken only by the big man's heavy breathing, until

211

Rollison said:

'Abbott shouted "Barbicue" for a dozen people to hear; that will help. Good, sound evidence to support the fingerprints, even if he tried to back out he couldn't now. It's never wise to make public statements. You'll have to warn him about that when he's in dock. Or ask your solicitor to. Who will you employ? Or won't you worry?'

'It was Abbott!' screamed Barbicue. 'You said so yourself, it was Abbott! I knew he was getting desperate; he was afraid you would find he was in it; he wants to get me hanged to save himself. I wouldn't have anything to do with murder. Abbott killed that policeman, too. I told him it was madness! I never killed anyone! I've never raised a hand against anyone in my life!' He stopped, but was sobbing for breath. 'Oh, dear God, this couldn't happen! It was Abbott, I tell you—Abbott!'

Rollison sneered.

'Abbott who killed Bennison, too? Didn't you want Bennison blamed?'

'I told him "no shooting, no killing"! Bennison could have been caught with the papers there. I was going to tell the police. I—'

Rollison said: 'Bennison would have killed himself, you hoped, just as Gerrard did.' Rollison stepped to the table and took a glass, helped himself to a finger of whisky and drank it neat. 'I needed that,' he added, flatly.

Barbicue was struggling for breath, and

212

Angela was staring towards him, not at the Toff. He was clawing at his collar, his mouth wide open. He was like that for what seemed a long time, until there was a tap at the door.

Rollison opened it, and saw Grice.

'Hallo,' he said. 'How long have you been here?'

'Long enough to hear the last part of the entertainment,' said Grice very slowly. He too was looking at Barbicue. 'Just long enough for that, no more.'

'That's too bad,' said the Toff, but his eyes were smiling at Angela. 'You wait until I tell you how we made him crack. That'll be worth hearing, won't it, Angela?'

He paused, then grew alarmed. 'Angela, it's all right, it's all over!'

But Angela slumped down in her chair.

*　　　*　　　*

Later that day Rollison sat in the lounge of 7 Braddon Place with Andrew Lane, Lady Gloria, and Angela. Jolly stood near the door.

'Yes, sir,' Jolly was saying. 'I followed Abbott to his Bayswater flat, and waited there until he was taken into custody. I am very appreciative, m'lady, of this opportunity for hearing exactly what happened prior to that. With your permission I will go to Gresham Terrace now. There is a great deal that needs doing.'

213

'Off with you,' said Lady Gloria.

Jolly bowed, and left. Andrew Lane smoothed his moustache and admitted that he was surprised, for it had seemed to him on the previous day that there was no case against Barbicue.

'There wasn't, either,' insisted Angela. Rollison smiled.

'No case until we made one,' he said.

'We? *I* had nothing to do with it. Rolly, I thought you really meant to kill him.'

'Haven't I?' asked Rollison.

'If there's one thing I don't see clearly,' said Lane slowly, 'it is the actual part that Bennison played. Was he a partner with Barbicue?'

'Yes,' said Rollison. 'Grice has heard it all from Abbott, now; he telephoned me. They worked together, but Barbicue had the lion's share, and Bennison didn't like that.' He smiled a little twistedly towards Angela. 'Sorry about that,' he added sincerely.

'I knew Bennison hated him, but I thought it was because of Father,' Angela said. 'I was pretty sure Bennison shot at him that day. Rolly—do you think he intended me to be blamed?'

'I doubt it,' said Rollison. 'In fact I think he suspected Abbott, and wanted him framed for Barbicue's murder. Then he would have been sitting pretty, with the evidence all against Barbicue.' He paused, and then went on: 'It's pretty certain that Barbicue *did* plan your

214

father's failure to save himself, you know.'

'Richard,' declaimed Lady Gloria, 'there is something I am not clear about. The letter which was stolen from this room. What exactly *was* in it?'

'If I have any more "Richards" I'll go sour on you,' said Rollison. 'There may have been a thousand pounds, to justify Abbott's first story, just in case I should open it. I'm not sure. There was nothing else. He told me there was, yes, but that was a red herring.'

'A red what?'

'You're not really as naive as that,' said Rollison. 'A red herring, or a fishy smell across the trail to send me chasing after the envelope and the motor-cyclist, and far away from Barbicue, to give Barbicue time to get things in better order.' He put his head on one side. 'I'd rather have a red herring than some kinds of salmon, wouldn't you? Aunt Glory, will you look after Angela for a while, until she's decided what to do?'

'Of course I will.'

'Thank you. I must get on to the flat, now I shall probably have to rejoin my unit tonight. My love to Aunt Matilda, and ask her not to do it again.'

He walked slowly to Gresham Terrace, whistling a little and thinking contentedly of Grice, who had telephoned a most generous apology. He entered the flat with his key, and on the spur of the moment telephoned a number in Aldgate. In a few seconds Lizzie was speaking, her voice echoing loudly in his ear, her words difficult to understand. They sounded like:

'I seen the pipers; the dicks never give yer no credit but I know 'oo did it, don't we all? 'Strewth, we don't arf owe yer somefink, Mr Ar! 'Ere! Sammy says 'op in an' see 'im if yer can, an' I won't say no this time!'

She laughed, and said much more, including the fact that she was 'all right because of the insurance'. Rollison replaced the receiver with a satisfied smile, and went into the kitchen.

Jolly was standing on a chair, and packing many things into the larder and refrigerator. In his hand was a carton of butter.

'Good afternoon, sir,' he said. 'I hardly expected you so early.'

'Jolly,' said the Toff, 'what is all that?'

'The contents of the parcel, sir. You will remember that it arrived the other day.'

'And you'll remember what I said was to happen to it.'

'Yes, sir,' admitted Jolly, stepping down with the butter. 'I cannot deny I remember, but since then the whole of the stores have been discovered, and thanks to you—entirely to you—there is no fear of any further outbreak on any grand scale. I thought that in the circumstances I would be justified in adding these articles to the larder.' He paused. 'Of course, sir, if you feel very strongly about it I

216

will repack it and send it to the police.'

'It was to go somewhere else,' said Rollison. He scowled. 'Halve it, Jolly. Send one half to some worthy cause, worthier than you and me, and do what you like with the other. There *was* some Louis de Salignac, wasn't there?'

'I hoped you would remember that, sir,' said Jolly. 'Yes, I have it here. I hope you will be able to stay in London for a few days, and have a well-deserved rest.'

'If I have much more to do with you,' said the Toff severely, 'you'll make me completely unmoral. Whatever you do, don't tell Lady Gloria about the hoard, or I'll be "Richard" for the rest of my life.'

We hope you have enjoyed this Large Print book. Other Chivers Press or G.K. Hall & Co. Large Print books are available at your library or directly from the publishers.

For more information about current and forthcoming titles, please call or write, without obligation, to:

Chivers Press Limited
Windsor Bridge Road
Bath BA2 3AX
England
Tel. (01225) 335336

OR

G.K. Hall & Co.
P.O. Box 159
Thorndike, Maine 04986
USA
Tel. (800) 223–2336

All our Large Print titles are designed for easy reading, and all our books are made to last.